RUDOLF TESNOHLIDEK

Translated by Tatiana Firkusny, Maritza Morgan & Robert T. Jones

Afterword by Robert T. Jones

Pictures by

MAURICE SENDAK

Farrar, Straus & Giroux

New York

THE CUNNING
LITTLE VIXEN

THE CUNNING
LITTLE VIXEN

Smooth white logs, and those damned thieves stole them right out from under my nose," snarled forester Bartos as he stormed out the door of the police station. His rage was gradually ebbing, the way a hurricane ebbs, but thunder still roared through the dark corners of his soul.

"Smooth and white as a woman's knee," fumed Bartos, "and somebody stole every last one. Didn't leave a splinter. Damned villains! If I catch one of those scoundrels, those thieves, I'll settle accounts with him and there won't be a thing left for the police and the courts. They only lock up innocent people anyway, dog damn it!"

The forester was furious, and no wonder: he had been hit by a double disaster. During a game of bowls at Pasek's tavern on the first Sunday of the season, while he had been thinking how the whole human race is dying of worry and malnutrition, he had thrown every last ounce of his strength into a powerful shot at the bowling pins. It was a terrific strike—dog damn it!—and all the pins had gone flying.

3

But one of them had sailed over the fence and headed straight for neighbor Svabensky's back yard. It zoomed right into the quiet wee, wee house where Svabensky was sitting, through the door-way that had lost its door during the war—nobody had ever bothered putting it back—and poor Svabensky thought Russian shrapnel was coming at him. Before he could collect his wits, the pin hit his pipe, snapped the stem, broke the mouthpiece, and knocked out one of Svabensky's teeth. The porcelain pipe bowl flew God-knows-where into the dust, and the top of the bowling pin snapped off at the neck with a shrill whistle.

Trying to patch things up with Svabensky, the forester had gone to town and bought him a new pipe, decorated with a pair of stags and a picture of St. Hubert, a pipe with a juniper stem less brittle than the original cherry one. But with Pasek, the tavern owner, things were not so easy. The forester had to promise him the best linden wood to replace all nine bowling pins, plus an extra piece for the broken one, and even throw in an offer to get game-keeper Blazek, who used to be a woodcarver, to carve them all just as if they were fine alabaster. All on condition that Pasek keep silent as a tomb about the accident. All the players had sworn silence with a handshake, but before the night was over, the whole village knew about it. The next morning every wife was warning her husband, "Listen here, old man, stay out of Pasek's—they're murdering people with ninepins in there."

Forester Bartos tried his best to end the gossip. He picked out a beautiful linden tree and had it felled, cut up, and stacked to dry. But before he could send the wood to Pasek, it vanished as utterly as if the earth had swallowed it. That was the last straw. Forester Bartos went straight to the police, though he hated to do it. Sergeant Venclik promised he would find the wood even if somebody had built a bed out of it, which cheered the forester

4

a little and set him on the road to recovering his good humor.

Now he was on his way home, passing Pasek's tavern and feeling thirsty. The sign with the stag's head looked so inviting! But how could he possibly face Pasek without having kept his promise?

He started to curse but stopped himself just in time. Lo and behold, there was the Reverend Father waddling along on his way to Pasek's, and he had spotted Bartos. Too late to avoid him. The priest and the schoolmaster talked so much that it would be all over town that he was ashamed to meet people.

"That really will be something, if they think I'm so dishonest I have to hide from them," thought the forester. Quickly he stepped forward and roared a greeting at the priest.

"Well," said the priest, "it's high time we saw you. We were beginning to think we would meet you again only on the occasion of your last rites. This isn't it, is it?"

"Not yet, Reverend, dog damn it."

"Well, well, *Deo gratias* that we are here. The schoolmaster is waiting inside, so for once the card game will be complete."

Pasek's whole place was rocking with laughter, and in a short while the three friends were deep into their God-pleasing work. The forester had a lucky streak tonight, ace after ace, and the beer was like syrup—you could stand a coin on the foam. The last thunder rumbled away into silence, and a rainbow arched radiantly across his soul. They say the wren builds the coziest of all bird havens, but tonight this inner room at Pasek's rivaled even the famous wren's nest. When the forester proudly announced "Closing with seven!" and the schoolmaster lost the game, the three toasted one another for the first, but certainly not for the last, time.

5

The sun had risen from its soft bed, washed its face in cold dew until it reddened, then primped itself into a beautiful day before the talkative trio finally decided to go home.

"That was a fine evening," said the schoolmaster expansively.

"Listen, Reverend!" roared the forester as they were leaving the tavern in high spirits. "Do you think we'll have that good a time in heaven? You know about things like that!"

"The eye seeketh not, the ear heareth not," replied the priest, adding with a twinkle in his eye, "But you'd better not bowl in heaven or you'll smash up the world long before Judgment Day!"

"So what! Just wait until I get those new pins made! They'd be finished by now if it hadn't been for those thieving scoundrels. Imagine! They stole my logs! Those logs white and smooth as a woman's knee! And you, Reverend, you know a little about knees like that, right? Dog damn it!"

"Ignoravi et nescivi corpus tuum, mulier," admonished the priest.

"Hey, teacher"—the forester turned to the schoolmaster, not bothering to address him in his usual formal fashion—"translate that for me. I might understand hunter's Latin, but I'm not so good at Church Latin."

"I know not and understand not your body, woman," said the schoolmaster, obediently translating the priest's quotation from St. Paul's Epistle.

"Oh, come on, Reverend! That might be true now—I believe you—but some twenty or thirty years ago I'll bet you were singing a different song, you old fox!"

Just then a mosquito buzzed piercingly next to the priest's ear, and he angrily slapped at it.

6

"Shoo! Get away, pest!" he cried, and in his anger stumbled and would have fallen if his two reliable companions hadn't caught him.

"That was a good stumble," noted the forester. "The Holy Book says our legs are weak and hurry toward sin. See, I remember some of it still." With sudden concern, he asked, "What's wrong?"

"A mosquito is after me," retorted the priest.

"Sure it is," laughed the forester. "Just a mosquito. I say it's a nice hangover. All our heads are spinning, and our ears are buzzing like a whole flock of mosquitoes!"

But it really was a mosquito. It circled again toward the priest and went straight for his hand, as if bent on kissing it. In a high, thin voice it was singing an ancient hymn, which nobody except the priest could understand.

Having renounced all ire,
Gluttony, worldly desire,
Live in honesty,
Sobriety, modesty,
Trusting in heaven.

"Trusting in heaven," repeated the priest in a low voice. He hiccuped.

"Some trusting in heaven," said the forester. "Trust wouldn't give you the hiccups. Our womenfolk are going to send us to hell, not heaven. I wish I didn't have to go home."

The schoolmaster solemnly nodded.

And the mosquito sang and sang. He was a very religious mosquito and had first seen the light of day in a mud puddle in front of Mechacek's tavern, nest of the Eagles and the Children of Mary, and the first flight he had undertaken in this world was into the back room behind the bar. He got there just as a young clergyman, timid but already disgruntled with the easy-going ways of the priest, was in the act of founding a chapter of the Third Order of St. Francis with a milkmaid and other persons equally well suited to that purpose. The impassioned eloquence of the young clergyman had enraptured the tiny mosquito and won over his humble soul to the best party, the one suitable even for animals: the People's Party. The mosquito had become more and more religious by the hour and finally sought his livelihood exclusively in religious processions. There he would sing along with the choir and watch over the morals of the young, not hesitating to pursue them into the remotest corners, where they went to hide from the eyes of their elders, and then to punish them painfully. It grieved him no end that the very people he was saving from sin invariably cursed him. Ignoring this, he eagerly and untiringly continued to visit the pilgrims' sleeping quarters like a guardian angel.

Today he was coming back from a pilgrimage to Krtiny. His moral guardianship had made him weary, for the boys had been chasing the girls worse than a swarm of young mosquitoes, worse even than gnats before a rain. But his fatigue left him now when he spotted clerical garb. He was charmed by the strangely wobbling, though dignified, walk of the priest, and by the childish attention of both his companions, and he thought to himself that these people were probably on the verge of becoming creatures of some higher species, for they seemed to hover like spirits in the air, moving above the earthly dust.

So the mosquito began to jubilate, stretching all his legs and both his antennae, singing happily and flying effortlessly, filled with bliss.

By now a bright day had dawned and the sun, its toilette

finished, entered like a glamorous beauty over the top of Baba Hill. The priest was obviously moved by the splendor of the morning, for he bent low to the ground, and while his friends held him like a babe in arms, he performed a ritual whose religious significance the mosquito did not comprehend. But suddenly the insect was seized with inspiration, and remembering King David, he intoned a psalm:

> *The mountains skipped like rams*
> *And the little hills like lambs.*
> *What ailed thee, O thou sea, that thou fleddest?*
> *Thou Jordan, that thou wast driven back?*

Before he could finish his song, the priest's face brightened, and with a lighter step, he marched on. At the crossroads the forester said goodbye to him and the schoolmaster, then headed off alone toward the forest.

10

The mosquito decided out of respect to accompany the two men to the parsonage. Carefully making no sound, he eavesdropped on their wise talk and tried to absorb all he could for his own enlightenment. He heard the priest proclaim as he entered the gate of the parsonage: "An excess in any form is harmful, I say unto you. And woe to you, forester, if you go to sleep in the forest. You won't wake up before noon." These words impressed the mosquito most powerfully, and he immediately decided to test the accuracy of that prediction.

The forester was headed for the Black Glen, where the air is always cool and fresh, where one breath is like a sip of healing water. The sun beamed hot, a thirsty oriole called, the newborn morning grew sultry, and as Bartos trudged he looked longingly at the peak of Baba Hill, wishing he were already at the top of it.

"We're going to have a storm soon," muttered the forester. He lifted his hat and wiped his forehead. His head ached and ached. "This heat would kill a horse. I'll just lie down and rest a minute. I'll tell the wife I was chasing poachers. She's a good woman, she'll believe me."

In no time at all he was stretched flat under a bladdernut bush on grass soft as velvet. A cuckoo over his head called out, a wood pigeon cooed, and a turtledove giggled like a giddy girl. The forester was filled with bliss in the coolness, among the sounds of his beloved forest.

"It's like the morning after my wedding night," he mused, already half asleep. "I was worn out just like now. And you, my rifle, my best girl, I can't leave you lying next to me like a walking cane. You've not grown old, you've not tormented me, you never grumble, you don't scold me for every mug of beer. Here's where you belong, on this old hunter's heart." He put his arms around his rifle as if it were a lover and was asleep in a second.

A woodpecker chopping away at the top of a fir tree stopped working. Hanging on to the trunk with his claws, he opened his beak in surprise and looked around for fellow woodworkers. He was hearing something that sounded like the whizzing of a bow saw. He would have gone to see who was sawing wood, but it was too much trouble to fly off and look, so he went back to work. But no matter how hard he chopped, no matter how much noise he made, he was unable to drown out the forester's snores, which rang through the glen.

The racket aroused even the blasé cricket who lived in a sand pile under the fir tree. Annoyed, he began to fiddle a fast cricket *galop*, and when he stopped playing to retune, he called his neighbor, the grasshopper, to join his music making. The grasshopper was perfectly willing, but she was a bit worried that the cricket, who was a distinguished musician, might object to her old-fashioned fiddler's trills. Reassured that today's concert was not an artistic event, she sat down under a goatsbeard flower and waited for the cricket's downbeat. An inquisitive blue dragonfly, that wandering melancholy beauty, flew in from his birthplace beyond the willow trees, and soon it sounded like the village feast at Ricmanice, where two bands play at the same time, each in its own tavern, trying to drown out one another (and when the bands don't have enough musical instruments to go around, they make do with mortars and graters until the whole village, even the belfry, shakes with sound).

The concert in the underbrush attracted the mosquito, who had finally said goodbye to the priest by breakfasting off his tonsure and was now on his way home. He was pleased to find the forester sleeping peacefully as a baby.

"Golly," exclaimed the mosquito, "a gentleman like him, and he's lying here in the weeds like a bum. He's probably afraid to go home and face his wife. I'm glad I'm single. I ought to spike him."

The mosquito had a strong dislike for humans who worked in the woods and interfered with the forest life. For one thing, country people usually reek of smoke and tobacco. For another, he once had sat on gamekeeper Blazek's hand: it was hard as a barn floor, and no matter how he tried, he could not get an honest drop of blood. All of a sudden, Blazek had slapped at him, and the mosquito escaped only because of Divine Providence. The gamekeeper's voice had bellowed through the woods: "Devil take you, you miserable pest! Don't you have enough beasts to eat that you have to eat men, too?"

This time, before attacking the forester, the experienced mosquito took care to determine the best landing spot and decided on the thick ear, partly because it would give him an opportunity

13

to lecture his victim. Ready for lunch, he cautiously approached the dark red earlobe, zeroed in, delicately wiped his stinger, and buzzed: "See, you sinful human, what can you do against me now?"

The forester emitted an inhuman sound. His throat whistled, his mouth opened, and he began to snore.

"Now you've got hiccups," snapped the mosquito, and poised himself for a sip of hunter's blood. But the forester's legs suddenly moved, his throat rattled, and his whole body abruptly rolled over.

"Golly! That's no good! He almost mashed me!" exclaimed the mosquito as he deftly leaped into the air. "Even a mosquito should have himself insured before he pays a visit to a wild man like this. Just you wait, daddy, we'll look you over and see where else you're soft. Ugh, you smoke! You smell awful!"

Examining the forester again, the mosquito decided that the safest spot for attack would be the nose. It is, after all, right in the middle, and no matter where the rest of the body goes, it never gets stuck in the ground.

"Bzzzz! Golly! Bzzzz!" sang the mosquito, and swiftly landed on the intended site. The nose was as big as a mountain and covered everywhere with swamps, spotted with cavities and pools like a mountain under polar ice. Wherever the mosquito touched down, tiny puddles formed around his feet, oily as metallic water in a meadow. He didn't think twice, but chose one of the many pools, bent down, and drank.

There was no blood in it, but it tasted good. The greedy mosquito hurriedly took several deep swallows. One pool smelled of cumin brandy, another of juniper berries, another of anisette with calamus, and the last had a strong scent the mosquito re-

14

membered from the past autumn when he had breathed it in at night near barrels of fermenting plums. He would have sat there drinking for hours if the forester's hands had not suddenly stretched out like a pair of monstrous tongs and scratched the nose at the very spot of the mosquito's feasting place. He barely got away.

How he did escape from the nose remained an eternal riddle to the mosquito. When he came to, he was lying flat behind a blade of timothy grass. He had almost broken his back falling on an anemone stem, and he ached all over. He tried to stand up but could not move.

A conceited young green frog, something of a dandy, hopped out of the den where he had gone courting and, looking at the mosquito in astonishment, said accusingly: "Say, citizen, what are you doing there? Aren't you ashamed to laze around here like a human? You look like you're drunk!"

"Golly! Hold me down or I'll bust up the place!" cried the mosquito. "I feel weird, like I'm in a tavern on a dance floor! I can't stand up!"

His body felt light as dandelion fluff. He staggered up and began to dance, spreading his mandibles and his front pair of legs.

"Tra-la-la-la-la." The mosquito danced, accompanying himself with a song. "Too bad you aren't a girl, sweet frog, we could dance together! Golly, I say . . . *HIC!* . . . play the song about the white flower! Don't move the floor so much, it's already tilting! It's . . . *HIC!* . . . going round and round!"

One of the mosquito's legs got stuck in a daisy, and he lost his balance and crashed onto the grass. The frog shook with laughter.

"Where are you off to?" mocked the frog. "If you'd stick to plain water, citizen, none of this would be happening to you!"

"Go home, foreigner!" shouted the mosquito, calling the frog

15

what the other citizens of the glen called him, for they all gossiped about the frog's being an immigrant: a sleepy fisherman had brought him here in his pocket from a poaching expedition to Lounek's trout hatcheries at Hylvaty in Bohemia.

"Golly! Shut your mouth . . . *HIC!* Where were you when the world was born? Golly . . . *HIC!* You stupid inflated balloon, you snot-nosed sack of green, you don't even know how to dance! You were black and yellow during the war, but now you pretend you're green! Now you're brave, but when all the fighting was going on, you were hiding in mama's den. I'll smash you one! There won't be snot left of you!"

In a blast of fury—the frog never did understand the reason for it—the mosquito started breaking flower stems and knocking down blades of grass. Finally, his fury vented, he fell down on his back and lay like a corpse. His head dropped and only by bracing it with his front legs was he able to hold it up, but his antennae went rigid and he could not manage to lower them. The green frog mocked him with vindictive joy.

"You're kicking and bucking like everybody else in that party you belong to. Every time there's a meeting, you shout that not even hell itself can stop you, but look at you now! You have been stopped! In my party, nobody is allowed to think the way he wants or say what he thinks. Everybody has to follow the party representatives and act according to party resolutions, because we have a very strict organization. At our meetings we all keep our mouths in the mud and pay attention to what the leaders are saying—Croak! Krrrr!—and when their throats get so dry they can't talk anymore, the rest of us lift our heads out of the water and all shout at the same time: Croak! Krrrr! That's right! Yes, indeed! Krrrr! Croak!"

"You dirty Bolshevik!" hiccuped the mosquito with much effort. "I may be suffering the torments of Adam, but at least I realize how beautiful the world is. It's turning, turning, round and round, and I'm turning with it. Man is the master of the world, and on the tip of his nose is paradise, and in paradise are paradisiacal springs! I am bewitched! My humble mosquito soul ceases to exist, and I am becoming human!"

He heaved himself up. His body tensed in a spasm, and opening all the parts of his mouth wide, he performed the same ritual the priest had on his way home from the tavern. After that, he felt both horrible and wonderful at the same time.

The frog was overwhelmed at this fantastic occurrence. Seeing the mosquito topple and fall into an ecstatic slumber, just like the giant human under the tree, the frog grew desperate to taste the unknown sensation himself. Quivering with excitement at the thought of such a new experience, he bounded straight onto the forester's nose.

He was nearly overwhelmed by the sultry heat and the heavy vapors rising out of the human's open mouth. Excited, but afraid of falling between those horrible teeth, he impatiently adjusted his feet on the nose and pressed his body eagerly against its tip. How it burned! It was exactly as if he were sitting next to a blacksmith's furnace.

The forester's head swam with colorful dreams. He dreamed he climbed and descended mountains—that he had even wandered to the North Pole, where the frigid air was freezing his nose. He shivered at the chill, opened his eyes, and, not quite comprehending, stared at the green frog.

"Dog damn it," he swore at the little animal. "Your legs are as cold as my wife's, and you're not ashamed to sit on my nose! It's enough to give me the grippe! You spotted fool, I'll fix you!"

He grabbed for the frog, and it barely got away.

The forester didn't know whether he was still dreaming, or exactly what was happening to him. He sat up and looked around, trying to remember where he was and how he got there.

"Oh yes, I remember. That sinful Reverend Father lured me to Pasek's, then he and the schoolmaster kept me drinking there till morning. Those scoundrels! The priest's housekeeper won't dare bawl him out, and the only female the schoolmaster's got is his bull fiddle, so I'm the one who's stuck. My poor old woman's probably wailing all over the place that poachers shot me. Maybe she's even got the police out looking for me. Bartos, you better rack your brains how to get out of this mess instead of just lying here in these weeds. A hangover is a heavy rider, and it's got you saddled good. Now you'll have to carry it on your own four legs!"

He carefully felt his clothes to make sure they hadn't been torn by his journey through the underbrush, then scrambled gingerly into God's daylight. The sun was high and nearing noon, its beams streaming through the branches, as Bartos, to his surprise, spotted a narrow trail on the forest floor.

"Look at that! A path I never saw before," he said with pleasure. "What kind of game goes here? After them!"

Nearby, on the slope facing Black Glen, a blessed fox family lay resting after breakfast. Mother Fox was snoozing because the baby, Sharp-Ears, had kept her up all night. Sharp-Ears was painfully cutting her eyeteeth, and with babies that is always a bother. By noon she had quieted down, but still she clung to her mother's fur as if it were a skirt and refused to have anything to do with her brothers and sisters.

"Mommy! Look! What is that?" whimpered Sharp-Ears. All the little ones—Black-Nose, Little-Tail, Feather-Catch—instantly stopped playing and crowded around the strange creature who seemed to have fallen out of the blue sky into their midst and was now sitting there breathless, eyes popping out as if it had just sprinted a mile. Sharp-Ears sniffed it.

"Oooo, it's cold!" she cried.

"And naked as a rock!" exclaimed Feather-Catch, surprised.

"It left its tail at home," added Little-Tail in wonder.

"Mommy, please," said Sharp-Ears in her most pleading tones, "is it good to eat?"

Mother Fox did not answer. She was grateful for the un-

expected arrival of the green frog: it would entertain the children
and she could sleep a little longer. The young cubs crowded
around the frog, wondering how to play with this curious creature. They all were so busy with their new toy, and Mother Fox
was dozing so soundly, that none of them noticed sinister rustlings
in the underbrush and the rapacious human face that appeared
like a wild beast among the leaves.

20

Forester Bartos watched the playing fox family for a moment, then thrust the branches aside and hurled himself into the scene, grabbing the nearest cub. Like a pair of tongs, his fingers clamped on to the tail of spoiled little Sharp-Ears, while Mother Fox and the other cubs fled wildly into the depths of the forest.

Sharp-Ears immediately recovered from the shock of capture and decided to betray no fear. Poor thing, she could not suspect that her future among humans would be hard, that many months of slavery and humiliation would pass before freedom, revenge, and happiness were to be hers again.

Forester Bartos brutally gripped Sharp-Ears by the neck and held her up like a puppy, examining his trophy in triumph.

"You young rascal, I'll blame it all on you! I'll tell my wife I was out stalking foxes and couldn't get home earlier. Too bad I couldn't catch the rest of your family! You do more damage than the poachers. You've got fleas, but that's all right—we've all got those, rich and poor alike. I'll hold you nicely and take you home. The children'll have fun with you!"

And he marched happily off with Sharp-Ears tucked under his arm, schoolbook fashion, through the wide clearing, toward his house. He wasn't worried any longer about his wife's tongue-lashing. Even if she was as mad as a hornet, she would melt, the way she always did when she saw that he had thought of grandson Pepik. Should Bartos choose to climb the tallest pine tree for a raven's nest or hunt all night and day for jays, domestic peace was assured if it all was done for Pepik's pleasure. Too bad the boy did not properly appreciate his grandfather's love, too bad he was such a troublemaker that, were he anyone else's grandson, forester Bartos would have flown into fits of rage.

21

Sharp-Ears put up no resistance during her trip. She stared at the passing landscape, the clumps of trees, and was amazed at the sight of open fields filled with the voices of peasants singing at their work. As they neared the forester's house, her heart began to beat faster.

She saw a human den, not too badly built. It had several holes in it, large and small, for entering and exiting in different directions—not even a hamster could have built better. Obviously the den had been occupied for a very long time, since it had a hard-packed path leading up to it. But there were no remains of feathers or skins lying around to indicate to Sharp-Ears man's fodder. Judging from the general appearance of the human carrying her now (the only one she had ever seen), she tended to the theory that man ate grass and clover like cows, goats, and deer, but a closer look at his teeth made her suspect that he might be carnivorous.

She was further startled when the human pulled out of his pocket a pouch made of the intestine or stomach of some animal, extended his mouth by putting a strange proboscis into it, and started to consume something foul-smelling. Soon he was puffing out blue, stinking clouds that circled around his nose. Sharp-Ears concluded that man is probably like a hyena, devouring not only dead bodies but dead souls as well. She decided to study the mystery later but, for the moment, concentrated on looking around outside the human den for leftover food.

There was none. Instead, she spotted something that looked like a big, comfortable bed piled high with straw and jutting up like an island from a shallow lake. Around it were more man-made dens, inhabited by animals, not humans. The little vixen did not know them all. In one of the dens she glimpsed a creature who looked almost as furless as a human, with large ears which he used to shade his eyes. He was lying down and panting heavily, and she guessed that he'd been stuffing his stomach at some feast in the big human den. Sharp-Ears decided that this animal, who kept grunting *"Oink oink,"* must be a friend of the humans, possibly one of their relatives.

A new revelation greeted her with every step. Down the wide, hard-trodden path a small human came running toward them. Sharp-Ears instantly guessed it to be a human cub. How ugly it was! It had only a handful of hairs on its head—probably it was just starting to grow its fur—though it was no longer blind. The top layer of its hide was crumpled, torn in places, and again there was no sign of fur anywhere. The most hideous part of it, though, was its legs: there was not a single good claw on its hind paws, and though there were claws on its front ones, they were very underdeveloped, and probably for that reason the cub had to hold them suspended in midair.

With the human cub came another small animal whose appearance confused Sharp-Ears so much that she was not sure at first whether or not it was a human cub, too. The tongue hung out of its mouth and was of good size, and it walked very nicely on all fours, but its legs were much too short and crooked. And its ears differed drastically from those of the one walking on its hind legs.

When these two small animals reached the forester and Sharp-Ears, they made horrible noises, and the four-legged one stood on its hind legs and shamelessly sniffed at Sharp-Ears in a non-human way. Caught in an embarrassing situation, she lowered her tail, for it is not necessary to express friendliness on meeting unwelcome and intrusive creatures. The forester laughed loudly and shoved Sharp-Ears at the cold nose of the four-legged nuisance.

"What do you think of that, Catcher! Isn't that something?" He roared so loudly that Sharp-Ears held her breath. The four-

23

legged Catcher, however, introduced himself to her almost in fox fashion. He sniffed her everywhere he was supposed to in a polite, well-bred manner, and Sharp-Ears thought, "He certainly acts intelligent. He is educated and not vulgar like a human. I must get to know him."

Forester Bartos cut short Catcher's demonstrations of politeness and stepped into the human den. Sharp-Ears instantly realized that her suspicions about humans were correct, that they indeed were far worse beasts of prey than hyenas. Skulls of bucks and stags hung in herds on the walls, gnawed so clean that there wasn't a grease spot on them. She shook with terror, thinking these human beasts would gobble her up in the same way. Her fear turned to panic when, for no apparent reason, the wall suddenly broke open. Out of the rift came an old, big human female. Sharp-Ears knew right away that she was not a male; no need to sniff her, her looks were so completely different. Her body was twice as broad as that of the male, her legs much shorter and hardly visible at all. Having uneasily examined her figure, the little fox concluded that she could not have had too many cubs, for she could not possibly have nursed more than two. But surely human cubs must drink a lot! More than geese!

Another detail confirmed Sharp-Ears's identification of the she-human: the female began to bark at the forester so furiously that he could not manage to answer. At home, Mama Fox had carried on just like that when her papa had come back late at night, singing and shouting, with his fur rumpled and torn, talking nonsense and refusing to say where he'd been. The old human behaved just like Papa Fox, who would pacify his wife by bringing her some rare catch, a hen or a duck, a partridge or a young hare. The forester planted his feet wide apart and proudly displayed Sharp-

Ears to the she-human while the little fox shivered all over with fear. The woman stared at him suspiciously for another moment, then stopped her torrent of talk and declared, "You're just bringing fleas into the house."

Still grumbling, the woman went out and returned with something Sharp-Ears had never seen before. It was a small hollow, carved from the top of a stump or scooped out of the ground, and brimming with milk. They placed it on the floor and coaxed Sharp-Ears to eat, but she was hungry and needed little coaxing. Catcher eyed her jealously and would gladly have helped her finish the milk if he had not been kept away by stern human voices. The human cub, its mouth hanging open, crouched beside Sharp-Ears and watched her every move.

And so it was that Vixen Sharp-Ears came to live with the forester and his family in their house. At first she was homesick. There was no one to cuddle up to, no fur to pull; it was like being in an orphanage. Happily, though, Catcher became her friend, a gentlemanly escort through the nooks and crannies of the humans' den. There was no end of those; not even her rich Uncle Fox could have afforded such living quarters. But she was happiest in her hiding place under the cupboard. Well fed, she would crawl beneath it, flirtatiously stick her head out, and listen with delight to Catcher's tales. The little dachshund would make himself comfortable on the floor and tell her funny stories.

He swore to her that he'd never been in love and did not even know what love is. He claimed he'd devoted his life to the arts and that at night he sang melancholy songs he himself had composed. But the forester, not understanding his artistry, often beat him cruelly for his singing. Catcher painted his lonely life in rich hues and described his tortured heart, which was especially filled

25

with pain in February and March, the months of love. He raved about brown eyes and an ebony-black nose, he praised the beauty of long ears reaching the ground and spoke of the splendid tail that during the dizzying laughter of blissful moments forgets to wag as he presses his love-heated breast against his lover's body.

Sharp-Ears listened to Catcher, at times deeply touched, then indifferently, according to her mood. Sometimes she feigned outraged chastity, and at other times she modestly closed her eyes and turned crimson under her fur. Catcher wouldn't give up until he lured her from her hideout. And when they both were feeling miserable and sad, they would invent some game or joke to drive their sorrows away. Often they indulged in a high-spirited frolic, with Catcher making up for his slighter strength by a show of affection. He would grasp her in an embrace and whine with pleasure when her nose tickled his neck. He would let her roll him over, and then he would snap at her tail with ardent, delicious bites. It was obvious that Catcher was just a puppy, a mere schoolboy in the ways of love.

Sharp-Ears didn't know much about love either. Her knowledge of the facts of life came from overhearing the arguments of a family of starlings who lived in a tree over her native den.

The starlings' married life was very disorderly, especially in the days before the new separation and divorce laws were passed, and quarrels and fights were a common occurrence in their nest. The couple accused each other of all sorts of immoral and indecent doings. From their shouting, Sharp-Ears gathered that the husband was a shameless philanderer, that he took part in all sorts of improper things that went on in the crown of the old beech tree, the meeting place of a rough bird gang that went there to get drunk on beechnut liquor. Several times the woodpecker had to come break up the noisy party, and then he would denounce the debauchers from the pulpit for all the forest to hear. After the rowdies received their week's pay, Police Commissioner Raven and his two deputies, the eagle owl and the falcon, often had to come and restore order at the beech-tree tavern.

The young starlings were no better than their parents. One of them was carrying on a sinful affair with a sluttish cuckoo who taught him to trespass on other birds' nests. Another was obliged to pay monthly alimony in the form of hazelnuts to a noisy magpie, and one of the starling daughters—an unsightly, dirty-looking thing—was having an affair with a young raven who was still serving time in the military. At the same time, she was going out with a screech owl who worked as a night watchman. Her aunt, a strict old owl, would often fly over to peck and berate her.

Sharp-Ears, bearing all these things in mind, kept Catcher's advances within limits. She let him play games, but her sharp teeth were ready to attack his throat any time he tried to go too far. If that failed to stop him, she knocked him down and rolled him in the dust. That shameless dog sometimes became very daring: once he even grabbed hold of her tail with his whole mouth. Sharp-Ears made such an uproar that Catcher crawled away to the rubbish heap, ashamed to the bottom of his soul. Seeing him repentant and genuinely sorry, Sharp-Ears went running to him. To prove she had a good heart, she curled up beside him and dozed off in a childlike embrace. But she kept herself alert and on the lookout for her maidenly virtue.

27

It wasn't long before Sharp-Ears felt like the mistress of the house. She had realized that Catcher was useless and totally green, afraid of humans and a complete coward—one whiff of the forester's whip and he would crawl into a corner or hide under the bed. Sharp-Ears was far more enterprising, decisive, and resolute in her actions, an emancipated female. If the family forgot to serve her breakfast on time, if her food was some uncertain concoction or a bit burned, she instantly went looking for something better. Before she learned her way around, though, she made mistakes.

Once, she spilled a plate of soup, although she quickly lapped it up anyway. Another time she jumped onto the bench by the kitchen stove and started to eat some strange human food. It was runny and sour, and Sharp-Ears had no idea that it was pancake batter, but once having started she refused to give up. Complaining bitterly of human ineptitude in the culinary arts, she stuffed herself until she was sick.

Another time the forester's wife took a roasted duck out of the oven. Beautifully cooked, with a golden crust, it filled the house with delightful smells and made Catcher drool at the thought of the bones. Sharp-Ears had no intention of waiting until the humans' noon mealtime. She decided just to sniff the duck, since the fear of getting a beating stopped her from doing more. So Sharp-Ears sniffed, and the smell was so fantastic that all her whiskers stood up.

"Leave it alone!" warned Catcher under the bench.

"Stop worrying!" hissed Sharp-Ears. "I'll just have a little bit of the leg!"

Never had her mouth tasted anything like it. Her head swam, and before she knew what she was doing, she had devoured the leg and dragged the whole duck under the stove. Catcher watched like an idiot, saliva dripping, but he was too terrified even to sniff.

"Come on," she coaxed him, "don't be scared. Have some. It's all right, we'll leave them the bones."

Sharp-Ears got a beating she never forgot. Next time she preferred, like Catcher, just to wipe her whiskers and stay away from whatever came out of the oven. Her appetite, though, gave her no peace, and she would rack her brain trying to figure out ways of getting at the kitchen delicacies without getting caught and punished. Otherwise, she felt perfectly content with life at the forester's house.

The courtyard was always full of chickens clucking and cheeping, so many that the forester's wife couldn't count the population. Sharp-Ears heard her tell the maid that there were "too many good-for-nothing roosters around here, and we ought to kill a few," so she immediately decided to help out. The youngest rooster was noisy, but he couldn't fly very well, and he couldn't outrun Sharp-Ears. She sank her teeth into his neck, his head went flying off, and soon he was nothing but a pile of feathers behind the

29

fence. Sharp-Ears felt pleased with herself and thought pityingly of her father, how long and hard he had to hunt before he could bring home even an old jackdaw to his family for dinner.

The only real problem Sharp-Ears had with her comfortable life at the forester's house came from the human cub, little Pepik, Bartos's grandson. The boy was like an eagle, and though he didn't actually hurt her, he was always pecking at her. He wouldn't leave her alone for a minute, waking her from pleasant dreams and sometimes even bringing along another human cub to help torment her.

"Look at this, Franta! Bet you don't know what this is!" he boasted, and held the squirming Sharp-Ears up by the scruff of her neck. "It's a fox! We got a fox!"

"So what!" retorted Franta. "She's tame. She won't even bite."

"I'll bet I can make her bite!" said Pepik.

Sharp-Ears tried to ignore them but swore she'd get even the first chance she got. Then the boys invented a game that sent her into a rage. Pepik held her while Franta jabbed at her face with a stick and both boys laughed wildly. Pepik wanted to try the trick next, but being more thorough, he stuck his stick into her nose. Sharp-Ears sneezed, and that made him laugh all the harder.

"Do you think I'll put up with this the way Catcher would?" raged the vixen. "I'm not a dog yet!"

"Hear her growling?" said Pepik, and Franta hit her on the nose again.

"Stop it!" growled Sharp-Ears, "or I'll get you."

Now it was Pepik's turn to hit.

"Cut it out!" yelped Sharp-Ears in her native fox tongue. "One more time and you'll be sorry!"

But the boys had no intention of stopping.

"Wait, let's get her with both sticks at the same time," said Pepik. "She's mad now, she's ready to bite. Watch out!"

Franta took his advice and hid behind Pepik.

"Now!" ordered Pepik.

Sharp-Ears bristled all over but only bared her teeth and opened her mouth warningly. Pepik, the grandparents' spoiled pet, grinned maliciously and hit Sharp-Ears on the ear with his stick.

"Now you've done it!" barked the vixen. "It's time to spill some blood!"

She flew at him like an arrow and, without stopping to think, grabbed his leg. She only meant to scare him a little, but blinded by anger, she squeezed her teeth together too hard. Pepik's pants shook with terror, and he screamed and cried.

"Aaaa! Aaaaa! I'm hurt! She bit my leg off! Grandpa! Where are you? Grandma! Come and help me! She's going to eat me! Franta! Help! *Aaaaa!*"

31

But Franta only stood there like a post, waiting for the fox to let go—Pepik thought he was an idiot and told him so later on—and Sharp-Ears realized she had lost her temper and that trouble was ahead. She hurriedly let go and dashed off to find a safe hiding place. Pepik's yelling and screaming drove her farther and farther away, and the farther she got, the faster she went.

Meanwhile, Franta had pulled himself together. "Stop screaming," he ordered Pepik, "or your grandpa will come out here and whip us. You know how mad he can get, and he told us to leave Catcher alone, even though all that dumb dog does is sit there like a dumpling. Your grandpa's going to send me home, and then he's going to beat you up."

Franta's words made remarkable sense to Pepik, so he clenched his teeth and suffered silently, like a martyr. His friend bent down, looked at the wound, and said knowingly, "You've got a big hole in your leg, but you'll be all right. At least your pants aren't torn. Come on, let's catch that fox and whip her good."

By now, Sharp-Ears had reached the gate, but she could still hear Franta's war cry. No matter how good her life was here at the forester's, a beating was a dismal prospect. She didn't have to think twice about what to do.

The forest was just ahead, deep and quiet, ringing with birdsong and humming with pine trees. Sharp-Ears felt a wave of nostalgia for the peace of the woods, for her home and her freedom. Forgetting all about full plates, she headed for the pine wood. But when she looked behind her, she wished she had bitten Pepik even harder, for the boys were right on her heels. They realized what she was up to and weren't about to let her get away.

"Catch her! Catch her!" the two were yelling.

Who on earth would try to catch a fox headed for the woods!

Not the roosters, certainly—not the hens! The swallows laughed, delighted with the race. A dung beetle climbed to the top of a pile of cow dung, the one that provided him with a comfortable livelihood, and held his stomach in merriment. A sleepy owl in the crown of a larch tree woke up and complained angrily that someone was always waking her, and it occurred to a squirrel

33

that a fox is not such an ugly creature after all and even knows how to use her tail properly when she wants to.

Alas, from the hour they were created, all females in this world have been plagued with curiosity. The reason Noah sent out the female dove to look at the flooded earth was that if he had sent a male, that male would have gone off looking for excitement and come back as ignorant as he was when he had left.

This ingrained curiosity was Sharp-Ears's undoing, and the reason for her return to slavery. She turned around to see what her pursuers were doing, ignoring the warning from a cricket, who shouted in vain, "Run! Run! Run!"

Disaster struck. She tripped—crash!—and there she was, lying belly up, with all four legs in the air. Shocked by her fall, she was also ashamed and embarrassed: a maidenly prude, she could not just get up and run on. The forest was only a few steps away, but no, Sharp-Ears carefully covered herself with her tail. Heaven forbid that someone might see what was not supposed to be seen!

Pepik and Franta rejoiced and, with one jump, got her. Sharp-Ears, still in a fit of modesty, was so upset about her tail and legs that she forgot she also had teeth. The boys easily grabbed her by the scruff and triumphantly ran back to the house with the fugitive.

The forester's wife met them at the front of the house. Seeing both boys and the fox so rumpled and dirty, and spotting Pepik's bleeding leg, she furiously shouted at her husband, who was repairing some traps: "Listen here, old man, I'm going to get rid of that fox of yours! She stinks and she gets in the way and the kids won't leave her alone! Besides, she's always making a mess."

"Then I'll tie her up," said the forester. And he did exactly that.

Poor Vixen Sharp-Ears! There she sits, tied to the dog-house, shamed and humbled. Even Catcher looks down his nose at her.

"You ought to have listened to me," he said condescendingly. "You shouldn't have stolen things out of dishes and tried to run away. Then you wouldn't be sitting here now."

The rooster called a general assembly of his flock, strutted around to show off his spurs and feathers, then delivered an instructive lecture to the hens: "Now you see how just, how wise, humans are. Without them, the world would fall apart. Our Miss Fox was chasing us and now she's sitting here tied up and not knowing what to do. That's because she doesn't lay eggs and sit obediently on nests. Go to work. Lay eggs. I'll be here helping you. People will love you."

The forester's wife seemed pleased with the rooster's sensible speech, for she came out and threw fresh grain to the hens. That's how things work among humans. Everyone knows that not even

35

a chicken scratches without a reason, and that those who crow the loudest and cluck the prettiest get the most grain.

Sharp-Ears nearly wept with rage. She clenched her teeth to stop herself from pointless swearing, then stretched out in the sun and pretended the rooster's insulting speech had nothing to do with her. Trying to contain her fury, she finally jumped to the top of the doghouse and curled up, everything inside her tense and crying out for revenge. She did not feel like eating and was not tempted by the dry potatoes put out for her in a dirty dish.

Meanwhile, the hens, roused by the rooster's inspiring speech, had organized an ostentatious march around the doghouse. One old hag of a gossipy hen clucked mockingly at Sharp-Ears: "Suffer! Suffer! You deserve it!"

Sharp-Ears left her alone as she waddled closer to the doghouse. She left her alone when the old biddy stuck out her craw in contempt, stretched her neck, and stood on tip-claws to see Sharp-Ears's face more clearly.

Only then did Sharp-Ears pounce, snap off the hen's head, and drag the body into the doghouse. The chickens went flying in all directions, and the proud rooster, fleeing, tripped and fell flat, like a war veteran hearing a gunshot.

Silence fell over the courtyard, and the feasting Sharp-Ears looked proudly around, as if everything belonged only to her. It felt good to wake up with a good appetite, good to go to sleep with a full belly.

It cannot honestly be said that chickens are endowed with great wisdom. When the Holy Spirit brought light to the world, He gave all His gifts to man and left the rest of the creatures in darkness. But even these hens were not so stupid as to scratch again under Sharp-Ears's nose. They stayed far away from the doghouse, completely ignoring the rumbling of Sharp-Ears's empty stomach. For a while she tried somersaults and various other entertainments to lure them closer, but they only looked at her with one eye and went on rummaging in the manure pile, out of reach.

Next she stood on top of the doghouse and made a speech. She spoke of oppression, of exploitation of the enslaved, of just punishment, and in the coda to her speech she offered to help the hens chase out the humans and take over the house for themselves.

"And who is going to feed us?" crowed the disbelieving rooster. "You?"

"Come close to me," said Sharp-Ears. "I will whisper it in your ear so that they don't hear us. If we discuss this aloud, man will beat us."

"That sounds just like you," said the rooster. "One minute you're full of courage, and the next you're afraid to whisper."

"Hens! Look at him! See what a leader you have!" scoffed Sharp-Ears. "See what an ugly, disgusting egoist he is! He wants you to satisfy his lust, and man gives him his miserable mercenary's pay for it. Demand equal rights! Abolish the old order! Down with false pretenders! Create a new world and a new society where all of you will share equally in the pleasures and happiness!"

"Without a rooster!" exclaimed one inquisitive old hen, who occasionally crowed and had other strange inclinations.

"What do you need a rooster for?" sneered Sharp-Ears. "He eats the best grain and makes you do all the work because he doesn't feel like doing it himself!"

"I'll peck you one!" shouted the rooster. "She wants to chase the humans away so she and her big hungry mouth can eat us all!"

37

He walked away from her, and the hens again dispersed all over the courtyard.

"I would rather die than live with such backwardness," Sharp-Ears called after them. "I prefer to bury myself alive!"

And she actually began digging a hole like a grave in front of the doghouse. Dirt flew in all directions. The hole got deeper and deeper, and Sharp-Ears finally disappeared into it altogether, tail included.

After a while, curiosity got the best of the hens. They fidgeted closer and closer to the pit, although none was brave enough actually to look down into it. Finally they rushed over to the rooster, called him a coward, and insisted that he look to see if the fox was really dead. A good-natured soul, he obeyed, fluffing up his tail feathers and stretching his neck as he sang a song to show the hens he was a knight without fear or reproach. Little did he know it was to be his swan song. He took off in a lofty parabola and set himself down at the edge of Sharp-Ears's supposed grave.

The vixen lay motionless in the pit. The rooster, a bit embarrassed, scratched with his beak under one wing and prepared to announce to his concubines that Sharp-Ears was dead. Suddenly the world turned black; blackness fell above him and below him as the vixen's mouth opened and her maw became the pit itself. All the hens could hear was the vixen's bloodcurdling laughter. Horrified, they fled into the henhouse.

From then on, the flock grew thinner and thinner, and Sharp-Ears grew fatter and fatter. Soon she liked being tied up more than she liked being free, and she began to dread the moment when she had finished off the last hen. But that was not to be.

The forester kept setting out traps for martens, but the traps

38

remained empty, and his wife looked gloomier every day. There were no more eggs. The courtyard fell empty as a graveyard.

Finally one morning, when the wife came out to feed the chickens, she met the last orphaned hen. The fowl's feathers bristled with fear, and she stood on one leg, clucking a mournful goodbye to the beautiful world. She missed the rooster and his gentle caresses. Not wanting to live without love, she had resolved to ask Sharp-Ears to put a fast end to her misery. There were tasty bugs and worms to be eaten, life in a family circle would have been wonderful, but now all was in vain. What's the sense in clucking when you know your eggs will never hatch?

The forester's wife looked at the lonely hen and her eyes filled with tears. She dropped her apron, letting the grain spill out, and turned to Sharp-Ears's house. It looked exactly like the old Jew's feather shop in the village.

"You slut!" she yelled, standing in the middle of the chicken cemetery. "This is what I get for not talking that old fool into making a muff out of you! Just wait, you miserable brute, I'll show you!"

Sharp-Ears flattened herself against the doghouse. Not that her conscience was moved—on the contrary. The old woman's lamentations only made her laugh, and she was merely pretending sympathy to ward off a thrashing. She barely suppressed a yawn, she was so bored. To the forester's wife it looked as if she was saying "Don't bother me."

That was all Mrs. Bartos needed. She ran toward the manure pile, shouting, "May I sink into hell if I don't get you with the pitchfork!"

Sharp-Ears leaped up and looked quickly around the courtyard. "It's now or never," she said to herself.

39

It was not easy for Sharp-Ears to leave the human den. She had forgotten how to fend for herself, forgotten what life in the forest was like. She had become tame, a slave, and it is never easy to exchange comfortable slavery for uncomfortable freedom, for freedom demands hard work and sacrifice. Even wise and sensible people find it difficult to break the shackles that bind them, and for a long time afterward they sigh and complain: "It was better when we had masters to take care of us."

There was not much time, and Sharp-Ears had to act quickly. With aching heart, she caught between her teeth the rope that tied her to the doghouse and, though it was of good prewar quality, resolutely chewed through it. She caressed the ground trodden hard by her own feet and with a great sweep of her tail waved farewell. Then slowly, moving reluctantly, as if undecided, she turned to the fence, jumped over it, and crouched in the nettles to see what would happen next.

The forester's wife rushed back armed with a pitchfork. She could barely see through her tears of rage; vengeance was roaring in her breast, and though normally of gentle disposition, she was bent on killing the fox. Broken dishes, spoiled lunches, Pepik's leg, devoured chickens—they all demanded ruthless revenge. She got to the doghouse and saw it was empty, with just a piece of rope left behind. In a frenzy, she dropped the pitchfork.

"Old man!" she shrieked frantically. "That animal will be the death of me! Shoot her!"

The nettles behind the fence rustled and a streak of rust-red flashed in a cloud of dust. Vixen Sharp-Ears was returning to freedom.

40

The forest looms dark, deep, and mysterious, or so it appears to people, especially poets and painters, who enter it alone. They feel sadness and sometimes even the kind of strange fear one feels in childhood: a fear of nothing. Couples, though, have another kind of fear, the fear of being seen. Old people can remember that feeling of being in love, two people lost in the solitude of the forest, but the young are in too much of a hurry to think these thoughts. Sharp-Ears felt a human's fear of the unknown.

"Where should I go?" she said to herself. "I'm lost, I don't know which way to turn. I'm sad. Why am I alone? If at least I had a roof over my head!"

Her playful mood was a thing of the past, and memories overwhelmed her. She even missed Catcher, clumsy as he was. If only there had been no pitchforks, no forester's whip! In the doghouse at least it never rained, and her dish was always full.

"Thunder and lightning!" she snapped, and punished her back

41

with a lash of her tail. "To think that a fox could be lost in the woods!"

Then she found herself in a clearing under open sky, and her gloom vanished. She was not alone. An animal personage was standing on a hill in the middle of the clearing, waist deep in a hole and looking very self-possessed. Arrogance radiated from every hair and bristle, from its posture, from the way its eyes turned up to the heavens, from its smug nose and the regal way it held its paws. Impressed, Sharp-Ears hid herself in the underbrush and wondered, "What kind of show-off is that?"

It was Mr. Badger, house owner, elderly bachelor, officious bureaucrat of the forest realm, now in retirement. He was dressed conservatively in ash-gray, with total disregard for current fashion; his attire made up in comfort what it lacked in elegance and was just right for the bulging belly he had grown after years of discerning gourmandizing. No longer politically active, he still upheld the family tradition by wearing whiskers to lend his face an air of aristocracy.

Mr. Badger had renounced the world long ago and now cared not a blink for social conventions. The reason was an unhappy love affair. Many years ago Mr. Badger had fallen in love with a beautiful otter from the Black Glen. That lovely miss came from a family famed for cleanliness: they washed every day, polished their claws, refused to tolerate mud between their toes, regarded a tidy house as the most important thing in life. Furthermore, they dressed very luxuriously: no human female will refuse an otter coat, and today otter hats still decorate the heads of the richest landowners.

Mr. Badger had courted Miss Otter diligently. He admired her proud bearing and her sinuous walk and her beautifully groomed tail, which looked as bewitching as a smile. She refused to touch ordinary food and would taste only fish. Mr. Badger was so carried away with her that he sometimes thought of writing poetry, but since his family tradition made him heir not only to a house and an aristocratic face but also to a remarkable insensitivity, he never made the slightest effort to please her otterlike tastes but paid court in accordance with his own wants: he presented Miss Otter with fat slugs and mice raised under hazelnut bushes, the kinds that have the tastiest meat, and he often dug up the finest maggots for her, the ones that melt on the tongue like Carlsbad wafers. For a while Miss Otter put up with his attentions, but when a respectable cousin, a military officer, came along, she made clear to Mr. Badger that she considered him only an old ass and went off with her relative.

Ever since, Mr. Badger had been a loner. He went on hunting mice and birds and slugs, but he kept them for himself. He sharpened his hunting skills and became a slave to his stomach, packing food into his pantry and, when the war came, branching out into the grocery business. His store became famous, and his belly became rounder. After he sold off or ate up his stock in the autumn, he slept lazily all through the winter. Since his trading had brought in a supply of tobacco, he took up the pipe and spent whole days smoking in bed.

The day Sharp-Ears fled the forester's house and returned to the wild, Mr. Badger had been on one of his rare outings. He had gone out to view the frolics of butterflies, mosquitoes, and dragonflies, but had sensed the barometer falling and judged that bad weather was ahead. When his corns verified those suspicions, he decided to take care of an important private necessity so he could stay comfortably at home during the coming downpour.

43

That done, he took one last look around before disappearing into his hole again.

Sharp-Ears, of course, was very curious to see where he had gone. Totally ignorant of the customs and manners of the forest, she had no idea how to behave toward birds, reptiles, and other

44

animals and, accustomed to rude human ways, went straight to the badger's den and stared in—back at the forester's house she had often seen gamekeeper Spacek peeping into the maid Anna's room while Anna was examining herself for fleas.

Sharp-Ears's jaw dropped in surprise at the sight of the badger's splendid den, with the badger lolling on his luxurious bed, smoking a long pipe. She could not stifle a gasp of amazement.

"Who's yapping out there?" said the badger, rolling upright.

"It's me, sir," replied the vixen politely.

"You beggar, you slut, you flea-bitten wretch! Stop snooping!"

"Hey, hold on there," retorted the vixen. "Don't talk to me like that! Your tongue is so lazy, even talking makes you sweat! Look at him! He's lolling around in a house big enough for three, and a poor thing like me gets yelled at just for looking at him! He's lazing there like a cow in a pasture, and he wants to chase me away! Just you try it!"

"I'll teach you to come spying around my house! Get away from here, or I'll call my lawyer and have you sued!"

"Sue this!" jeered the vixen, scornfully lifting her tail at him.

Forgetting his laziness, the badger grabbed a broom and hit her so hard she felt lumps leap up behind her ears. Startled, she fell into a patch of briars that scratched. Then, gritting her teeth in fury, she sat up and started hurling abuse. A farm wife at the Brno cabbage market would have envied her eloquence.

"Foul mouth! Tyrant! Dictator! You're as bad as Slosarek the murderer! What did I do that you had to hit me? Was I in your way, you piece of filth? The forest isn't big enough for both of us? You won't even let people walk by your slimy windows? I ought to take you to court, but you're not worth the bother. I'll tell you something, though, I'm not through with you! I'm going straight to the housing commission, and they'll decide if you

45

can treat people like this! When they throw you out, you'll find out what it's like to be without a roof over your head!"

Shocked, the badger tried to ignore her. He felt weak. "Let her alone. Nobody can outtalk a female," he said to himself, and relit his pipe.

The vixen wasted no time. Thinking of the luxury apartment and how much time she would spend going from one authority to the next, trying to oust the badger, she decided on direct action.

"You can't fight the rich," she thought. "That badger would have lost his house long ago if he hadn't bribed everybody."

By now, the noise had attracted the neighbors. The swift was jumping around in an ash tree, telling everybody in earshot that the badger was an evil sort, a war profiteer who had grown rich and arrogant. Before the war, declared the swift, the badger had only one pair of pants to his name, and he wasn't going to be allowed to abuse poor females any longer just because they had the audacity to stop in front of his house.

Sharp-Ears listened proudly to this show of sympathy and knew just how to express contempt and avenge herself at the same time, and in a most memorable manner. She squatted comfortably, lifted a leg, and began bombarding the badger.

"Here's something for your noble head, old gray whiskers! And if that's not enough, I'll send down some more right away! Go ahead, pick it up and start a new profiteering business with it. I'll use your mansion as a—well, I'm too much of a lady to say what. You better wear kid gloves for the cleanup. You might get some of it under your nails, and they're too fine for such stuff!"

Her revenge made her feel immeasurably better, but the badger down in his den felt terrible. He took off his cuffs, rolled up his sleeves, and began the nasty job of cleaning up.

46

"Pick up every piece and blow on it! It's so hot it'll burn your hands! You're so good at that you could get a job in Brno cleaning streets. They'd be glad to get you! Got any blisters yet?"

Down in his apartment, the badger worked until he was drenched in perspiration and had a stitch in his side. All his snobbery, even his dignity, was gone.

"That piece of trash—immoral riffraff," sputtered the badger. "She threatens me with the commission, calls me names, and then makes my apartment into—pardon me for saying it—a public lavatory. I'll wait till she's gone, then I'll board up the window."

He cleaned out the last remains of the vixen's revolting revenge, then lay down on the bed, filled his pipe, and tried to think, blaming himself for not having moved a long time ago.

He could have built himself a beautiful home under the maple trees on that sunny slope overlooking the river valley and the road that runs from the forest to the watering place. He had lived by himself long enough, and at certain hours that road offered a lively spectacle, especially when lit by fireflies. A stag with sixteen-point antlers would promenade there, side by side with a young doe—a refined old sinner with elegant manners, he was like an actor who changes girlfriends every week. Amorous young martens would rendezvous there. A repulsive skunk, smelling like a wine distillery and known for his habit of sleeping in the most disgusting places, would come there and make a nuisance of himself begging at doors and, when justly rebuffed, would pollute the air. Young hare dandies came to show off their flashy fur coats and their cotton tails trimmed in the latest fashion. The hamster, an insatiable miser and glutton, would struggle up the hill, puffing, the pouches of his cheeks stuffed to bursting.

"Maybe I should get married," said the badger out loud, still

47

lost in thought. "Something sweet and female wouldn't be so bad after all."

"Who'd have you?" came a mocking voice above his head. "Your pantry may be full, but you're stupid as a shoe. Here's something female for you, a present from me!"

The badger froze. Before he could move, he was soaked from head to heel. Not even in the worst rainstorms had he ever been so wet. Shocked, he looked up and saw Sharp-Ears posed in a delicate squatting position, just like the fighting stance of a Lisen market woman ready for heated combat. He barely managed to protect his pipe from being inundated. This was beyond belief. Had he owned a revolver, he would have shot the vixen then and there. He nearly had a stroke from righteous anger.

His moral sense outraged, the badger got up, looked around his beloved room, and resolutely spat on the floor. Even his slippers were full, and his food supply was completely ruined. Shaking his fist at the window, he was about to jump up and pursue the vixen but changed his mind just in time: chasing trash like her around the forest would only add to his disgrace. He might even be accused of hooliganism and harassment. It would be the end of his good family name.

"I'll move out," the badger decided. He dried the tears in his eyes, collected and packed his belongings, looked around for one last time, and left the house. He stopped at the doorway, not knowing which way to turn, while on top of the hill Sharp-Ears crouched under a juniper bush, shaking with laughter. The badger sniffed in contempt. On the slope above the glen he will be better off, much better. No such dubious characters will dare to come around, he will have peace, he will have his new house finished before winter sets in. Proudly he lifted his nose into the air and, not considering the fox worth even the most contemptuous glance, courageously set out for the tall trees of the deep woods.

Sharp-Ears waited until he had vanished in the underbrush. Then she trotted back to the empty den. She gathered some dry grass, mopped the place clean, waved her tail in triumph, sang a cheerful song, and settled into the soft bed. For the first time in her life, she tasted the delight of private ownership. This morning she had been turned out by humans and was on the brink of despair. Now she is the owner of a house, and the woods all around have become her hunting grounds. Under the larch trees are rabbit warrens. Doves live on the rocky slopes. Everywhere there is plenty.

Don't be afraid, Sharp-Ears. Your life here will be beautiful.

Before long, she slept as if wrapped in cotton. For the first time ever, she was sleeping in her own home.

49

Another summer almost gone," sighed forester Bartos as he tramped through the quiet village toward Pasek's tavern. Already it was September and the hot weather was past, not to return until springtime. The sun shone pale and weak, its slight warmth welcome as eiderdown at bedtime. Gossamer spun through the air, and the woods blossomed in yellow and red, the wind blowing through the crowns of trees, cold as spring water scooped up in bare hands.

It was the time of year when all villagers make the pilgrimage to the shrine at Vranov and to the fair afterward. The forester had sent his womenfolk, and only Anna the maid was left in the house. Bartos was sure the family would be back late, and he intended to make the most of his freedom: he had been unable to go to Pasek's tavern since St. Anne's Day two months before. That day the pilgrims' procession from Bilovice had ended up at Pasek's as usual, and the gamekeepers—Svabensky, Jedlicka, Mensik, even Bartos's colleague Folkner—had not been able to believe their eyes when they saw old man Pasek's new bowling pins. They were the pins Bartos had promised, made of wood as smooth and white as a woman's knee and standing there tall and beautiful like candles on an altar. Even now the thought of his astonished friends and neighbors made the forester laugh.

Whistling cheerfully and feeling pleased with himself, he burst into Pasek's tavern. In spite of the approaching autumn, which always makes old people feel melancholy, he felt so young that he almost feared his own high spirits.

The priest and the schoolmaster had been counting on him to come. They greeted him enthusiastically, and before a quarter of an hour had gone by, they were busy playing cards, as always. Their talk and laughter and the sound of cards slapping on the table thundered in the vaulted room. After an especially good game, their merriment increased until the ceiling shook. The schoolmaster was in such a good mood—the long summer vacation having made him peppy—that he even burst into song. First, accompanied by the priest, he sang the old student song *"Gaudeamus igitur,"* then delved into new songs—or new as far as this remote country region was concerned. One of them, about a maiden named Veronika, he had to repeat three times while the priest put on an innocent face and pretended he didn't understand, which greatly amused the forester.

After reflecting a bit, he turned to the priest and said, "Reverend, aren't we going to have an important wedding around here? Horses prance the hardest when the flies are thickest. Don't you think that someone's put a saddle on our schoolmaster here?"

The schoolmaster blushed and said nothing.

"Non des mulieri corpus tuum," said the priest, as if burying the schoolmaster's youth.

"You sly fox, tell us who you've caught," demanded the forester. "You wouldn't turn red as a cherry without a reason. And you, Reverend, stop plaguing me with your Latin. Every

51

time you start with it, things turn out bad for all of us. Just remember that time last spring!"

"Non des mulieri corpus tuum," repeated the priest with emphasis.

"I don't understand one damned word," muttered the forester.

"It means: You shall not give your body unto a woman," translated the priest, for the schoolmaster showed no inclination to help.

"Of course he won't, not any longer. Do you call that ladder a body?" The forester lifted the schoolmaster's coattail and pointed at his physique, scrawny and dry as a chip of wood, looking very much like a ladder made for plucking fruit from trees. To escape becoming the butt of all jokes for the rest of the night, the schoolmaster hastily changed the subject.

"Women aren't the worst things that can happen to foresters," he declared. "I hear you brought home a fox last spring. How did it work out?"

"Don't remind me about that fox," said the forester, frowning. "She got the best of me, that monster, and I don't want to think about her. I was glad to get rid of the beast. But to say that foxes are smart animals is not true. A fox can do a lot of things, but in the end even a fox goes crazy."

"May you be spared God's punishment," the priest reprimanded him. "God alone knows with what gifts He has endowed every creature. You may yet have to pay for your impudence."

"I'd just like to see it! A fox is smart only as long as it isn't in heat. Just like man. Look at the schoolmaster here! He is a wise man, but look at him now! Instead of playing you the ace of spades, he played it to me! Schoolmaster and teacher, you sing songs about the maiden Veronika, but I suspect that some maiden

Veronika is going to be singing songs about you! Even you will go crazy. A married man is no longer a man. He is only half a man, and caught in a trap. It is the law of all creation that we all get caught in the end, and it happens even to the fox, as smart as it is. In my opinion, marriage means the end of reason, even for foxes."

53

"And do you really know what marriage is?" asked the priest.

"Better than you, Reverend," snapped the forester. "After thirty years, I feel it in every limb. That's marriage, dog damn it."

"Marriage is the seventh sacrament," the schoolmaster pointed out.

"Perhaps. But I say it's double stupidity," exploded the forester. "See for yourselves! The reverend sits here drinking, and when he gets home nobody says a word. The schoolmaster could stay out for three days and it would be all right. But me? I went to sleep in the woods that day last spring, and a mosquito bit my nose, a frog jumped all over me, and to top it all, I even took a fox home—for shame!—just to have something to stop my wife's scolding. But think of this. Catcher! Come here! See? This is my dog, and what a dog, dog damn it! Faithful, clever, obedient. If this canine soul were in the body of a woman, then I'd want to be a widower this very minute. Tonight I'm not afraid of the trip home. He'll lead me there all right."

"As for that fox, you'd better heed our words," warned the priest.

"The devil take her, damn it. There's nothing to heed. She ran away, and that's that. I'm not going out looking for her. I wouldn't even think of it," growled the forester. "And what about you, schoolmaster, you're getting the cards mixed up again, devil take you! Looks to me like some woman has turned your head! You're playing like a sleepwalker. You know what they say: Lucky at love, unlucky at cards."

The schoolmaster tried to defend himself, but this time he could not escape an unpleasant discussion. The forester would not leave him alone, the priest teased him, even innkeeper Pasek nagged him.

"Listen, gentlemen," said Pasek very seriously. "I hear that the schoolmaster is having a new suit made. And what a suit! Yesterday, master tailor Svehla brought a piece of the cloth to show us. How many years has it been since he bought a new suit? And now! It must be because of a bride!"

"Will you please leave me alone?" begged the schoolmaster. He got up from the table, walked to the window, listened into the distance, then raised his finger and announced mysteriously, "The rooster is crowing."

"Never mind the rooster," rumbled the forester. "Because of a rooster, Peter denied Christ."

"I mean, it's time to go home."

"Home!" laughed the forester. "You don't sleep that much, dog damn it. There's a skirt waiting somewhere along your path home!"

The schoolmaster did not wait for him to finish. He paid his bill and walked out into the gloomy night. What else could his friends do but follow him? As they stood outside under the fading stars, the forester raised his hand to heaven, pointed to the sky, and said: "Schoolmaster, you Judas, why are you in such a hurry to get away from the tavern? It seems to me you'd rather sell your old bones to a woman than to the moneylender. Do what you want, but you'll be sorry, believe me. You'll be tearing out your hair, what little you have left. Mocking tongues say that God created women out of dogs' tails, but that's a lie, my friend, a big lie. Have you ever seen anything genuine on a woman? Neither have I. Teeth, braids, rosy cheeks, sometimes some other things, too. Everything false and nothing but false. But have you ever seen a dog, one single dog, with a false tail?"

The forester paused briefly and went on with his lecture. "No again. There you are. And have you ever seen a woman lead her husband home from the tavern without nagging? Such women, my friend, have never been born. 'In the sweat of thy face shalt thou eat bread,' said the Lord to Adam. Right, Father? But not a word about drinking. If He had just mentioned that we'd always drink in fear and anxiety, the first man would have divorced the first woman and that would have been the end of mankind. Here, see my dog? He'll lead me like a guardian angel all the way to my bed. That's what a woman is like, and this is what a dog is like. Come here, Catcher, let's go! You are a dog above all dogs, dog damn it. Farewell and good night, gentlemen!"

Having said those words, the forester ironically tipped his hat and directed his steps toward the woods.

The schoolmaster also tried to direct his steps. But how? And to where? The path tonight seemed to be winding twice as much as on other nights, and the earth had grown much rounder, for he kept sliding off it. "Either my center of gravity is mobile," he reflected, "or the earth is rotating from west to east. Something is wrong tonight. Why did I spend the night in a tavern among strangers? Why did I stay up when the whole world has gone to sleep? Do I need to be looking for the way home in the dark, hoping I don't sprain an ankle? Damned path, the rain has washed it out again. None of this would be happening if I had stayed home. But alone? That's impossible. It would be different if I had some company—some nice, homey company."

At this moment he found himself at a fork in the road. A white path branched off, leading between garden hedges to neat houses.

"If I had no cane, no support at all, I would never make it

home," reflected the schoolmaster. "Two legs and a cane—that means three supporting points. A body supported at three points has the best distribution of weight. In other words, stability. Balance. Well, let us try it without the cane, just to test our stability. Damn! I'm going to fall!"

And he realized that his balance, whether supported by two points or three, was extremely unsteady. His body skidded now forward, now backward, and he decided he had better move closer to the fence alongside the path.

"Physics is an experimental science," he mused aloud. "Therefore, why should I not experiment? Newton discovered the law of gravity when he saw a falling apple. But tonight the earth is turning, if not in the wrong direction, then at least in several directions at once. I wonder what new sort of gravity I'm about to discover."

He lifted his index finger to his forehead, relying upon his feeble legs as two supporting points, for his soul felt as light as if it were being borne on the wings of butterflies, and he whispered softly: "The gravity of the soul! Let them make fun of me! I admit I love her! If I could see her now, I would confess my love to her, I would pledge my life to her, I would swear to take her for my honest, wedded wife."

Suddenly he was overcome by a rush of feeling and thought it prudent to rest again on his tripod. The wind rustled in the bushes—so tenderly, so lovingly it murmured in the twigs.

"Staccato," sighed the schoolmaster ardently, and the musician within him began to stir.

The breath of wind whispered away, and in a second the branches vibrated with a new and mysterious shiver.

"*Flagioletti!*" he moaned in a low voice, his excited fingers running up and down the length of his cane as if it were the neck

of his beloved double bass. He felt bewitched. When he finally lifted his eyes, he froze with astonishment. Among the branches, in the dark, he saw the vague image of a face peering at him from beneath a bonnet. Was it a ghost? An apparition? Was it reality?

It was she. And in her presence, he felt himself a miserable sinner.

"Terynka!" he cried, overcome with emotion. "Terynka! You here?"

Among the dark leaves, the face lowered itself closer to the fence, as if to see him better and hear his words more clearly.

"I am turned to stone, Terynka!" he began anew. "If I had known that I would meet you here, that you were waiting for me, I would not have stayed so late at Pasek's. I would have left those two drunkards hours ago. Speak to me. Tell me that you aren't angry to see me out so late and in such a state!"

The mysterious creature gracefully shook its head.

"You love me, Terynka! And I have been in love with you for so many years! Twenty-five years now since first I saw you! My fate is in your hands, and I wait for your answer!"

To be on the safe side, he rubbed his eyes. Yes, what really stood before him was the image of the sedate, circumspect co-owner of the big sweetshop which she and her brother had inherited from their parents at the peak of its prosperity.

"Forgive a feeble man burning with love," he mumbled. "I shall come to you, I shall hold you close in my arms, if you so desire."

The head in the bonnet moved shyly away from the fence.

"She is making room for me," thought the schoolmaster. "Who knows what else she will expect from me tonight!"

He quickly arranged his clothes, remembering that, as an

60

absentminded bachelor, he often neglected details, such as a button here and there, which might prove embarrassing to delicate ladies. Swept by a storm of passion, the schoolmaster dropped his cane and ran toward the fence, intending to swing over it like a young man.

Disappointment struck him like lightning. The dull face of a huge, overripe sunflower stared at him from among the foliage, and the schoolmaster, unable to stop his momentum, stumbled and executed the best somersault of his life around his own axis, to the sound of breaking slats.

When he got up and pulled himself together—and this took quite a while, because a man who is orbiting himself on an orbiting globe is not far from getting his head twisted around altogether—he observed sadly to himself while bidding farewell to his unattainable vision of marital bliss: "Physics is the true science of all truths. Even the gravitational pull toward a woman's heart is due primarily to inertia. It makes us fly toward emptiness, but even a stupid fence and a bump on the head are enough to make us stop. All right, so I got hit on the head, but just in time. It takes some people years."

It was a thought worthy of a great philosopher, and it consoled him quite a bit, but he could not completely overcome his melancholy as he continued on his way, with considerably fewer detours, to his bachelor apartment. He was still bewildered, and many things appeared to him upside down—and no wonder, for he felt as if his feet were up and his head down.

"Damned keyhole," he cursed when he got to his door and vainly tried to unlock it. His hat flew off during his struggle with unintelligent, inert matter, and as a precaution, he propped himself with his cane and inspected the lock closely.

"What am I to do?" he complained bitterly. "My key points up and the lock points down and I can't possibly turn the lock around. That would take till morning."

He held on to the door handle, thus preventing his wobbling body from falling, and also unwittingly restoring his stability of spirit.

62

"Wait! I don't have to turn the lock around, I can turn the key!"

And lo and behold, the door opened.

How good his bachelor's home looked. What a pleasant welcome to find his faithful companion, the double bass, standing humbly in the corner. Even the tepid water in the jug tasted like a splendid beverage.

In this topsy-turvy world, getting undressed required painstaking effort. "What was I doing last night!" Scolding himself bitterly, he went on: "Do I have the right sleeve on my left arm, or is my right arm in the left sleeve? The shoes are correct, quite correct, one on each foot. But I might mix them up, too, so I'll take them both off at the same time. There! Step down with the left and pull with the right."

The bootjack is the quietest, most peaceful component of a human household, so long as nobody willfully upsets its balance—which is exactly what the schoolmaster did. Remembering the apparition of Miss Terynka, remembering how he had pursued the phantom, he said to himself, "To rush at her like that was the foolishness of a schoolboy. Suppose I had taken an elegant approach, holding on to the fence like this . . . and . . ."

But the law of gravity now was stronger than the law of inertia had been before. Table, lamp, jug, matches, candle, everything went scattering to the floor in wild confusion, just as the schoolmaster himself had done earlier. This time, though, as his foot slipped violently out of the bootjack, he fell onto the soft, fluffed-up bed.

"And this might have been my wedding bed," he whispered, his eyes misting with tears. "That is, I mean, if she—Terynka—had really been there. And if only I hadn't fallen on my head."

63

"Memnestho aner agathos einai," grumbled the priest to himself after he left his companions. "Remember to be a good man," he added, translating the Greek. "Bless me, what classic is that from?" He thought about it, and it all began to come back to him. When he had encountered those words for the first time, he had been a very young man, a student. He had carved them into his school desk as a motto for his future life. Back then, he had wanted to become a good man and an actor—not just *some* actor, but a romantic idol who would break hearts as if they were walnuts. To love, to love all the time, that's what *aner agathos einai* meant to him in those days.

And now?

"Now all that's past. Now you're standing here like a broom in a corner after it's swept up the floor when the party's over. *Aner agathos einai!* Of course! I know what that's from. Xenophon's *Anabasis.* We get old, our memories fail us."

And the priest, leaning on his own tripod of umbrella plus two legs, just like the schoolmaster at about the same moment, and still pleased with his memory, tried to light his cigar. He tried and tried, God only knows how many times he blearily tried, but it absolutely refused to burn, like a factory covered by high fire insurance. He exerted all his strength puffing, but at that moment the relatively most secure leg of the tripod failed him: his umbrella slipped, and the priest sat down suddenly on the hard ground.

"Never mind, there's no fire," he comforted himself. "One can also think while sitting down. How many times did I once sit just like this, but not alone? She had hair like gold, heavy and shiny, and her eyes were innocent, puzzled, as if she didn't know what the world is all about."

Even now the priest could imitate the way the girl looked, that tender gaze that used to stab him to the heart. Long, long ago it was. As the young "Father Alois," and only half faithful to his motto, he used to act in plays with the local youngsters, in touching, harmless dramas with titles like *On the Farm and in the Hut.* Those happy days had ended when a girl named Marie became pregnant by a butcher's apprentice, who violently denied the whole thing and tried to foist the blame on Father Alois.

Her eyes had been like mountain pools, with the blue skies reflected in their depths, hiding the treachery and treason that lay even deeper, like a slimy bottom.

"I thought she was a flower on a slender tree, a chaste Susannah at her bath—and they blamed me because I had not sinned. From that time on, I've not been able to look at any woman with pure thoughts." And for a long time the priest sat, lost in contemplation, unable to mold his thoughts into words.

"Good Lord! I can't keep on sitting here!" he suddenly realized. "I'm right in front of cobbler Nesrsta's house. An unpleasant character, that one. Nothing on earth could make him understand that a man's life is a fragile vessel. He'd describe me nicely to the newspapers, I'll bet!"

He tried to get up, then sagged to the ground again, struggled some more, and finally managed to get to his knees. Still on all fours, he grabbed his hat, which had rolled away, picked up the cigar, which, amazingly, had started to burn as calmly as a stick of incense, and after a few attempts achieved normal human posture. Drenched in perspiration and exhausted, with a heavy head and eyes closing all by themselves, he stumbled toward the parsonage. When he finally reached the threshold, he was worse off than the schoolmaster, for he had forgotten his key. So he lifted his umbrella, banged on the door, and then threw himself against it with all his weight.

"Open the door!" he shouted. "Open the door!"

He hoped desperately to escape those memories of a wasted life, which seemed to pursue him through the darkness of this night like vampires. His faithful housekeeper, familiar with her master's habits and still awake from a pain under her left shoulder, heard the blow on the door and rushed downstairs to unlock it. Fully dressed and looking thoroughly unseductive, she hurriedly undid the latch. Before she could stand respectfully aside, the door burst open and the priest tumbled in, landing in a heap on the floor at her feet. The cigar didn't even fall out of his mouth, although he kept feverishly mumbling words in a language unknown to the housekeeper.

"Memnestho aner agathos einai!"

The housekeeper burst into tears at his pitiful condition. "Those sinful companions, that schoolmaster and the forester, they've been at him again!" she complained furiously. She dragged the

66

priest away from the doorstep, locked the door, and with super-human effort pulled him into the bedroom. With her own hands she undressed him like a child and, blushing and modestly turning her head, retied the string of his underpants so they would not fall off, and then put him to bed.

"Now, then," she said, "how does that feel?"

"Good. Ah, so good," sighed the priest. Calmed at last, he fell asleep.

Memnestho aner agathos einai. Remember to be a good man.

67

E asy now, Catcher," forester Bartos begged his dachs-hund as they wobbled through the village toward the open fields. The Holy Trinity in its shrine at the edge of the fields looked at this unrighteous pair disturbing the sacred peace of the night, and it seemed as if the sandstone lips moved gently in a smile. The forester looked around and, reassured that no one else was in sight, went on talking to his faithful dog.

"The Good Lord created the world in perfection, but He went wrong in one thing, Catcher, and that one thing lost us paradise. It was woman, dog damn it. Just count, Catcher. He created the whole world in six days. On the seventh—Saturday, according to the Jews—the world rested. And then, on Sunday, there was man walking around the Garden of Eden talking to animals just like I'm talking to you right now. But you know something? Sunday is a lousy day, disgusting, endless as the ocean. I can just imagine how that man felt—no taverns, no friends, no card games, no nothing!

"And pretty soon he'd had it up to here talking to animals. I mean, Catcher, what am I going to talk to you about for a whole day? Or to some sheep or donkey or elephant? So the man got sad, and he ended up with woman around his neck.

"God created the woman to brighten his days. But the woman was a Sunday job, and you know how good Sunday rush jobs are. Today you don't find anybody working on Sundays except now and then a shoemaker. But women, they've got Sunday in their blood, and that's why they're all the time putting on the dog, dog damn it.

"And the man saw the woman and he went crazy. Crazy seven times over!"

During the forester's speech, the faithful Catcher had ceased wagging his tail. Now he stood still and growled.

"Hush, friend. Shhhh. I mean no blasphemy. It's just my loud mouth, me talking to make the trip shorter. Hush now and lead on. It's still a long way home. But I'll tell you this. If I'd have been in the Garden of Eden, I wouldn't have uttered a sigh for any woman. It's good for man to be alone. A woman's not worth nearly as much as one good dog."

Catcher, unappeased by such flattery, growled louder.

"Because everybody who's a man—I mean, a real man," the forester went on, "starts to go crazy at a certain time, in spring, when May comes. And man isn't the only one. Every creature has its own time to go crazy, even a fox."

By now, Catcher had heard enough lecturing. He suddenly jerked the leash out of the forester's hands and went tearing straight across the open fields.

"Come back here, you bastard!" shouted the forester. "Get back here!" But Catcher paid no attention. Barking wildly, he ran on as fast as he could.

69

"There's a reason for it," thought the forester. "Catcher wouldn't bark so hard without a reason." The forester tried to think. Finding that difficult, he got out his pipe and lit it. With a bit of smoke under the nose, it's always easier to think.

"Dog damn it, I'll bet that's our vixen. Blast me to hell if that's not her hanging around here."

And true enough, it *was* Sharp-Ears prowling through the field. She had spotted the forester and heard all too clearly what he had said about her going crazy, for like most people who spend more time outdoors than under a roof, the forester talked very loudly. Insulted by his words, Sharp-Ears crept closer to hear more. The mention of her going crazy made her so angry that she lost her usual caution and forgot that the forester was carrying a rifle.

"Just you wait!" she growled. "We'll see. I'll show you who's crazy. I wonder which one of us is going to be the sorrier."

By now she was talking out loud, and at that moment Catcher caught her scent and ran toward her, glad to meet his old friend. He would have caught up to her if the forester, angered by Catcher's desertion, hadn't pulled out his whistle and started blowing it as if he had lost his mind.

"Will you come back!" he was screaming. "You think I left the whip at home, but I haven't! Look here!"

Poor Catcher knew he was in trouble. He shrank as if trying to sink into the ground between the rows of potatoes, then started to crawl on his belly toward the master. When he saw the whip, he expected the worst. As a precaution, he pulled in his tongue, put on his most innocent face, and prepared to lick his master's shoes should he change his mind and take pity on him.

But man would not be man if he had pity. The forester, though swaying uncertainly on shaky legs, grabbed the leash and began to whip Catcher unmercifully.

"So that's how you are! You'd leave your master behind? Dog damn it, that's what I get for trusting you more than a woman! In spite of everything, a woman's still a *little* bit human! Is this how you pay me back for all my trouble?"

The blows rained down on Catcher. The poor dachshund lost his head just like the forester and, trying to dodge the blows, spun around his master as far as the leash would let him. But there is an end to everything, even to a leash. The poor dachshund was choking, and his tongue was hanging out, and his howls echoed through the fields and woods. He remembered Sharp-Ears and how she used to laugh at his cowardice, how she had chewed so heroically through the rope that bound her to the doghouse and to the forester's dwelling, and he decided to follow her example, to end his enslavement to humans and join Sharp-Ears in the forest. After a particularly sharp blow, Catcher jumped up, exerted all his strength, and tried to wrench himself free of the forester.

The forester, already dizzy from Catcher's spinning him in circles, lost his balance and fell flat. He wasn't hurt, because he fell onto something soft, namely Catcher. And at that moment the poor animal thought his time had come. He screamed with all his might, the leash gave way, but Catcher no longer thought of running off. He simply could not move. Finally he sat up, checked his back to make sure it was in one piece, and began howling without letup.

"I'll disgrace him in every part of these woods and fields," thought Catcher, "and every animal will know how cruel man is."

The forester felt no better than Catcher. Though he was more shocked than hurt, his back was aching, his head swimming, and sweat was pouring down his face. Sitting there, he swore shamelessly. "Goddamned devil, goddamned pig of a dog!"

By now it was getting light. Dawn was breaking behind the hills, and it also dawned on the forester that he could not go home in such a condition. Disheveled, rumpled, and tired, he limped to the edge of the woods, laid himself down on the soft grass, and was asleep in a second. He slept soundly on this autumn morning, just as he had earlier, in the spring.

But this time the pious mosquito did not come, for he had died of old age. The green frog did not hop about. No fox family sported nearby. Instead, Sharp-Ears, older and wiser, gazed at him from beneath the bushes.

"Now you see who's crazy," she growled, "who went crazy even without a woman. You need a woman right now!"

She was pleased with Catcher. The dog sniffed the forester, stood for a while in confusion, and then, disregarding proverbial canine loyalty, slowly edged away. Limping on all fours, Catcher headed for home.

Summer went by, autumn went by. Frost came with bleak, short, unfriendly days and soon snow covered everything, betraying the footprints of animals. The forest fell silent, as if all life had died. Hares grew thin, partridges turned shy, the amorous, fashion-conscious pheasants ceased trysting in fields of tall clover. Now hunger arrived.

Sharp-Ears, scrawny and ill-tempered, spent whole days lying in the den she had inherited from the badger, thinking of her blissful life at the forester's house. Every memory was accompanied by the picture of the forester insulting her with his words about a fox going crazy.

"Surely I *have* gone crazy," she would say to herself when, waking up late in the evenings, she would go up to the entrance to look around. Yawning from hunger and fatigue, breathing on her feet to warm them, she would try to think how to rise above her situation. Though hunting seemed pointless, when night came she would fluff up her winter fur and, on shaky legs, feebly set out toward the glen and its rabbit warrens, hoping some hapless creature would let itself be caught.

It was nearly Christmas when, once again wandering unhappily through the glens and clearings, she reached familiar ground. There, beyond the larches and firs, stood the den of the humans, the forester's house, its roof covered with snow and its windows dark. Only Catcher's voice could be heard, barking idly. Tears came into Sharp-Ears's eyes, and she fiercely cursed her freedom. Wasn't she better off before, lying under the warm stove and sleeping under the cupboard? Even the time she'd been tied to the doghouse with that disgraceful rope didn't seem at all bad—not now.

As she was thinking those gloomy thoughts, a familiar voice broke through the still, freezing night, a voice that both comforted and irritated her. It was the rooster, the successor to the old, more cautious one; waking from a dream and still drowsy, he crowed out though it was barely past midnight.

Sharp-Ears remembered a hole in the wall of the courtyard and did not hesitate. "Ho, ho, ho, Sharp-Ears! Tonight you'll eat like a rich lady. Don't be afraid! Just hope that dumb Catcher's asleep!"

She squeezed through the hole and glanced cautiously at the doghouse, then eagerly at the henhouse. Catcher was fast asleep, like a born night watchman, and the pig was snoring happily in its sty under the henhouse. Nothing stirred in the courtyard. Sharp-Ears leaped forward, flew up the ladder, and expertly opened the henhouse door.

"Stupid people, they don't even know enough to buy a good lock!" she muttered, then slipped in.

Inside, it was as stuffy and smelly as a public tavern. Sharp-Ears spat in disgust as her feet sank into a thick layer of chicken droppings. The hens were sitting in tidy parliamentary rows on their perches, heads tucked under their wings, tails spread like negligees. The rooster's beak sagged open. Even in sleep he had the stupid look of someone in love, as if making love was his only mission in life.

"Get going!" said the vixen to herself. She snapped her teeth, and the headless rooster went sailing out the door. She expertly selected a few more young chickens to go after him—who would bother with tough, dry hen meat, fit only for city folk?—and when she discovered that she had more than she could eat immediately, she jumped out and began tugging her booty behind the courtyard wall. Three bodies she had to leave behind in the courtyard, for she had overestimated her strength. Finally she sat down at the edge of the woods and treated herself to a feast, then celebrated by launching into a noisy song that woke Catcher in his doghouse. That done, Sharp-Ears waved her bushy tail, gathered up the rest of her loot, and raced for home.

Catcher had no idea that it was his former friend who had awakened him. He had caught her scent and sniffed her trail, but because he was sleepy and lazy, because in winter he always overstuffed his belly in the kitchen, he didn't recognize who had been there. Not even the sight of the dead chickens in front of the henhouse supplied a clue to his sluggish brain.

The rooster was still warm. Catcher looked toward the house, but everybody was fast asleep. Knowing that the forester's wife never cooked at night, Catcher naïvely concluded that the rooster had been laid out for him. He didn't much care for chicken meat, but he couldn't resist licking the dead rooster's bleeding neck.

Catcher's sinful, careless act did not go unpunished. In the morning, while he was still lazing in his doghouse, he suddenly heard the forester's heavy step and his furious voice.

"That goddamned dog! He's got feathers all over his snout

like a gypsy chicken thief. Come out of there! What's this new trick? Who taught you this, you bastard? Who!"

Before Catcher could hunch himself down in a submissive posture at his master's feet and point out the vixen's spoor, the forester had grabbed him by the collar and was whipping him mercilessly across his poor back. The dachshund screamed as if he were being skinned alive. Even naughty Pepik was upset by this execution, because it vividly reminded him of bitter moments from his own past.

As Pepik turned sorrowfully away from the doomed one, he spotted fresh footprints in the snow, much bigger than any Catcher's paws could have made. He quickly pointed them out to his grandfather, and the forester let go of Catcher, ashamed even to look at him. The poor dachshund sat there, his back stinging and swelling, crying bitterly. This, thought Catcher, was even worse than the time they had been coming back from Pasek's tavern last autumn. The forester leaned over and carefully examined the tracks. No doubt about it. It was a fox.

"I'm an old ass, beating the dog like that. If that animal had human intelligence, I'd die of shame. Dog damn it, if he was as smart as I am, he wouldn't take a crumb from my hand—he'd mess on my shoes, that's what he ought to have done ages ago. Stupid as a stone, that's what I am."

A good look at Sharp-Ears's tracks restored Bartos to cold reason, and after a while Catcher saw him in the shed, loading his rifle. This was beyond Catcher's understanding. Eyes popping out of his head, he crawled to the forester and would have humbled himself before him if he hadn't been so ashamed.

"Is he going to shoot me?" he wondered. "If that bullet is for me, let him see that I am not afraid of death and will stand straight so he won't miss me."

But seeing the forester so gloomy, with his whiskers hanging down and his eyes squinting as if fighting back tears, Catcher was struck by another idea: "His conscience has overwhelmed him. He's going to shoot himself because he has been so inhuman to me!"

Catcher felt so sorry for the master that he even let a tear drop. What more can a dumb animal do, seeing the sorrow it has caused, sorrow driving a tortured human being to a desperate deed? Or when the human's mate, a being so worthy of love, so emotional, capable of shedding tears over a dead canary, calmly watches her lover prepare for suicide and accepts his despair with the expression of a singer receiving a bouquet of flowers? Then, when the forester's wife burst into tears, Catcher's conclusions were confirmed and he all but wept himself. In his simplicity he never suspected that husband and wife were only grieving for the dead chickens. That fact did not occur to him even when he jumped up on the forester and ardently began to lick his hand to avert his self-destruction. He barely escaped a powerful kick.

Catcher spent the rest of the day in a state of confusion. He was no wiser when, later on, he saw the forester's assistant, apparently on orders from the forester himself, set a trap at the hole in the wall. In his excited state of mind, though, Catcher soon forgot all about the trap, which later proved a calamity for him.

Night came, clear and moonlit, frost crackling the
shingles on the roof. Everything froze except the
smelly moat around the manure pile in the middle
of the farmyard. Thanks to the steaming pile and to
the cows' untiring efforts to replenish it, the temperature in the
lake seldom sank below freezing point.

Catcher was surprised when the lights in the house didn't go
out at the usual time. Did it mean that Anna the maid was
expecting her lover? Was Pepik ill? Or was the forester's helper,
Celestyn, that sullen character who never spoke, writing a love
letter or catching up on the bookkeeping?

The mystery was soon solved. The forester came out dressed
in an old fur coat drooping to his heels, the one he used for sleigh
rides, wearing warm house shoes and an ear-hugging nightcap
under his hunter's hat. He had on his gloves and was carrying a
rifle.

Catcher shook his head at the sight. The master never dressed this way to go hunting, not even for snipe. But the forester wasn't going far. He pulled up an old barrel next to the manure pile and sat down on it.

"I've got it!" thought Catcher. Full of joy, he wagged his tail and raced to the master. Touched, the master patted the faithful dog, and the two began to understand one another again. Catcher looked up at him as if he understood, and the forester, index finger raised in emphasis, commanded: "Watch, Catcher, watch! I'm not sleepy, but if I should fall asleep in spite of everything . . . well, your back's suffered twice already because of that vixen. But don't worry. We'll settle our account with her tonight. You've got to watch close!"

Catcher knew that the master never wasted words, and that he wasn't wasting them this time, for in a mere quarter of an hour the forester was as sound asleep as if he were home in bed instead of sitting outdoors on a freezing barrel. He no longer cared about the shame of having a fox stealing his chickens with impunity. His head rose and fell rhythmically, the rifle in his hands swayed to and fro, and Catcher worried that he might start his usual snoring and alert Sharp-Ears or, worse, accidentally make the gun go off.

Catcher determined to keep his promise at all costs, to keep it as a real man would, not because even real men sometimes fail to do that, not because he was eager to prove that a simple dog is better than the sort of man who gives his word but does not keep it, but because he hoped to see Sharp-Ears punished the way she deserved. Catcher wanted to do his part in helping to restore peace and security to the forester's house. Tail up, ears high, he ran silently around the farmyard, darted in to examine the garden, carefully sniffed the air, did all he could to merit the master's

79

praise. His swollen back provided further incentive to stay awake.

Meanwhile, Sharp-Ears had given in to her appetite for fine food. In an excess of generosity, she had left last night's loot to the crows, martens, and other rabble who had nothing to put into their mouths, and now she badly craved fresh chicken again. The sight of the lighted windows put her on alert, but she soon relaxed and crept toward the familiar hole in the wall. There her eyes caught sight of a strange object sticking out of the snow.

"I smell human mischief," she said to herself, and sat down to think things over. She remembered various hunters' snares and tricks, but it took her a while to figure this one out. When she finally did, she laughed, pleased with herself, and said, "A trap! That's what it is, a trap! They've recognized last night's visitor and set it out for me. I'd be some fool to walk into that. Never!"

The moon slid behind the clouds. Mysterious darkness enveloped the landscape and the house; the forest murmured gently, softly, as if whispering, and the wind tiptoed through the trees, making sure they were all sleeping and their winter dreams were tranquil. The vixen felt a cold chill. It flashed through her mind that it might be better to give up the expedition for tonight and go home. But immediately she felt ashamed.

"They'll think the vixen has gone crazy," she scolded herself. "Go! Go and cough in the faces of old Grandpa and that sniveling dog!"

She cautiously circled the house, at first slowly in a moderate trot, then in a fast canter. With one jump she leaped over the wall and landed in the garden. Carefully planting one foot before the other, she slipped along the fence, looking for an easy spot to crawl through.

Something rustled on the other side of the fence. It was the sound of short, waddling steps that, on a human scale, might have been those of a fat baker. Sharp-Ears strained her eyes and ears. It was Catcher making his rounds. He was marching along, military fashion, counting "One-two-one-two" under his breath, his tail up like a lance, head held high with all the dignity of a fireman in charge of a fire hose, a completely stupid expression on his face. Sharp-Ears was so sure he wouldn't notice her that she insolently marched alongside him all the way to the gate.

"I wonder if I should look in the garden, too," thought Catcher. He timidly cast a sidelong glance at the gate, and there the eyes of the two former friends, now enemies, abruptly locked.

"Beat it, you idiot," snarled the vixen, arching her back and preparing to pounce. "Stay away from me unless you've brought a bucket for your blood!"

Catcher, feeling safe as long as he was within range of the forester's rifle, positioned himself so that he could retreat with dignity, and snapped, "Smell that? That's your grave being dug!"

Sharp-Ears instantly realized that Catcher was trying to trick her. This poltroon pup was suddenly showing off like a German general. Tense silence hung between the two deadly foes. Then, through the silence, the vixen heard an unmistakable sound. "*TweeeeOOOOOFF!*" whistled the high-pitched tone, followed by a loud bass snort.

Sharp-Ears laughed and grinned from ear to ear. "Which one are you guarding, the pig or the old man?" she said derisively. "Has he got a stomachache?"

Catcher barked furiously.

"And now I'm going," said the vixen calmly. "Watch out and don't fall over your own ears."

She turned to go, when a devilish idea entered her head. "I'll get this idiot dog shot by his own master! Or else I'll land him in his own trap!"

81

To distract him, she barked: "You dirty hound, aren't you ashamed to stick your nose up a woman's skirt like that? Get a good look and don't go blind!"

Keeping a steady distance between them, she trotted along the wall, and just as she was passing the henhouse, the forester woke up. He had no time to take aim. A shot rang out, a bullet whizzed through the air and smacked into something with a loud *plop*. Before Sharp-Ears could look back, the night was rent by a terrific crash, a loud splash, a violent curse from the forester, and a long, piercing scream that hung shivering in the cold air.

Two disasters had struck at once. The forester's old rifle had a powerful recoil, which he was used to but which greatly surprised the aged barrel on which he was perched. The dried-up old barrel collapsed, its staves fell apart, the hoops slipped off, and the forester, losing his balance atop the wreck, fell backward into the stinking manure lake. The liquid was not frozen, but it wasn't very warm either. He sank all the way in, his old fur coat sopping up the muck like a sponge. The rifle filled up, too, and so did the forester's fuzzy slippers, which instantly grew heavy as hundred-weights.

The forester used to be an excellent shot, the best snipe hunter in the district, but there are moments when life plays tricks on us. When we are young it makes us follow the phantom of woman, but as soon as we come within reach, life sticks out its tongue at us—the woman belongs to another, and has for a long time. The closer we come to old age, the easier it is to fool us, and we are helpless objects in the grip of chance, like marbles in the hands of boys during springtime games.

Chance had played its own game with the bullet from the forester's rifle. The bullet whistled cheerfully, high above the farmyard, as if intending to disappear somewhere in the treetops, but instead hit the gutter, ricocheted, sped through the pigsty door, and scored a direct hit in the heart of the pig.

The pig, having been forewarned by a prophetic dream, was just scratching its back against the wall. The blue eyes of the innocent animal filled with tears at this human treachery that had denied it a natural death by the butcher's knife. The pig lay down on its side and uttered a long, dismal cry for its wasted life so prematurely ended, for in a few weeks it had hoped to tip the forester's scales at five hundred pounds. Its death scream resounded through the quiet night just as the forester sank into the fetid depths of the lake and just as the fatal bullet, having carried out the assassination, fell apathetically into the soggy manure pile.

Teachers and professors who are fond of telling their pupils touching stories illustrating the proverbial loyalty of canines, upholding them as an example for man, must be relying on very old and worn-out examples. The loyalty of dogs is purely mythical; in reality, a dog can be as utterly disloyal as man. Or, rather, isn't a dog faithful to his master only in the way that courtiers, mistresses, moneylenders, and pious subjects are faithful to the ruling classes? A dog is simple and stupid, but suppose it could come up with some such neat principle as people have: "Render therefore unto Caesar the things which are Caesar's; and unto God the things that are God's." What a perfect guardian of the house the dog then would make: smart enough to let the master feed him but permitting a thief to take the things that are "his."

Catcher forgot all about the supposed loyalty of dogs. Transformed into an athlete bent on breaking all track records, he flew after the vixen, and neither the forester's curses nor the pig's death cries slowed him. The fox knew how to handle him: she kept tickling his face with her bushy tail, like a girl showing her knees, and when Catcher's heart began to burn with the desire

83

to embrace her, all of a sudden her tail would smack him smartly on the nose. At last, with a demonic laugh, the vixen bounded onto the garden wall.

"Anything else you want, you muddleheaded mutt?" she called down to him, then waved goodbye with her tail.

"I'll get you!" wheezed Catcher, and flung himself at the hole.

Blinded by his lust for revenge, he had completely forgotten about the steel trap, and by the time he remembered, it was too late. Uttering a heartbreaking howl, he rolled over with his rump up and—the final straw—at that very moment Sharp-Ears stuck her head through the hole, exactly like a maiden looking out her window to watch a handsome man walk down the street, and mocked him unmercifully: "Don't cry so hard, little doggie! That trap was meant for *me!* It was your own fault you fell into it! I'm sorry to be in a hurry, but your master will help you! He'll be here soon! Have a nice wait!"

She lifted her paw and blew him an elegant kiss, waved her tail once more, and danced off down the path toward the woods. Catcher, fainting with pain, ground his teeth as he heard her barking a merry song: "As I was marching . . ."

"Damn you, bitch!" he shrieked.

When he came to, he thought it was raining and he must be lying directly under a drainpipe. But it was only the stinking mess dripping down off the forester's hat and fur coat. Freed from the trap, Catcher's paws hurt so much he could barely touch them to the ground. His whines and moans filled the frosty night.

The two luckless hunters headed miserably back to the house, the forester looking more like the king of some water sprite's realm than a human being—dripping wet, with his rifle leaking like a hose after a fire drill. Behind him, poor Catcher limped and wept with every step.

The house knew no peace for the rest of the night. The forester had the chills and, as linden-blossom tea didn't seem to help at all, he reached for a bottle of old plum slivovitz. He didn't drink to induce perspiration and thus ward off a cold; he literally rinsed his insides, for his entrails seemed clogged with manure, worse than an old sewer pipe. Swearing and cursing, silently and out loud, he consigned the vixen to all the devils of hell and solemnly promised that, should he ever get her, Sharp-Ears's skin would be made not into a muff for his wife but into a rug, which then would be installed in that certain small room where even after her death she would have to endure the same sort of suffering she had caused him that night.

Poor Catcher sat next to the bed. The forester's wife had tenderly dressed his front paws, but what was the use of that when he couldn't lie down? After his strenuous evening of guarding and chasing, all he wanted was to lie down and rest. And his poor paws would not let him.

So he sat up as humans do, trying to accept his fate like a man. Having lived all his life among people, and having acquired some of their wisdom, Catcher came near to succeeding. But, alas, his tail was in the way.

Every morning when the forester's wife stepped out of the house and into the farmyard, the pig greeted her with joyful grunts. Although she didn't come to see it every day, it knew perfectly well that she was the one responsible for all the extra tidbits in its food, and by this morning salute showed its gratitude.

But the morning after that eventful night, the pig was silent.

"Ungrateful brute," she thought, "that's because it got whey instead of milk yesterday."

She coughed to get the pig's attention. The pig didn't respond.

"I'll bet Anna fed it too much yesterday, and now it's sick," she fumed. "Nobody can depend on that girl. Anna! Anna! What did you feed the pig yesterday?"

"Slop!" sassed Anna from the cellar, where she was sorting vegetables.

"Did it eat all right?"

"As right as any pig eats. It was pouring out of his ears and his eyes. It made me sick just to look at him."

"When your boyfriend's slopping up liquor like a pig, you don't get sick, I'll bet!" retorted the forester's wife. "Well, something's wrong with it. It hasn't uttered a sound today!"

"Then go find out for yourself! It never would talk to me anyhow. Besides, no pig's going to order this maid around!"

Enraged by the maid's freshness, the forester's wife picked up the bucket of feed and started for the pigsty. The closer she got, the more worried she became. Finally, with deep foreboding, she opened the door. The pig was lying there, a cold corpse, legs up in the air and a look of martyrdom around its snout. She clapped her hands in horror and screamed.

"Jesus and Mary! Anna! It's dead!" she wailed.

"Oh, Christ, what will the master say!" called Anna, pretending to be upset, too. Coming up from the cellar, though, she threw back her head defiantly. "Serves you right," she muttered. "I'm not about to raise it from the dead."

The forester's wife happened to glance at the door and caught sight of a large hole. She looked at the pig and saw a matching hole in its side. "So that's what happened! That's why my old man's hiding in bed!"

She stormed into her husband's bedroom, shook the forester awake, and yelled at him while he struggled to open his eyes: "You old fool! You shot the pig last night!"

"What pig?" he mumbled. "The correct term is black boar, not pig. I haven't seen a black boar around here in twenty years."

"Not a boar! It's our own pig you shot!"

"Look at me!" moaned the forester. "Isn't it enough that I'm so sick? Let me sleep. I feel miserable. You can tell me when I get up."

"You ought to be ashamed of yourself! You go out to shoot

87

a fox and you kill the pig!'' But the forester didn't answer. He had gone back to sleep.

"That damned slivovitz," she said in a fury. Then she shouted for Anna and told her to run into the village and fetch butcher Farlik, who had been slaughtering the family pigs for years.

"Tell him to drop everything," she ordered Anna. "Tell him to bring the knife, the sharpening steel, everything he needs for butchering except the long knife for sticking in the heart. Tell him we can start steaming right away. And don't either one of you say a word to anybody about what's happened. Your master would have a fit. Also, stop at the school and the parsonage and ask the schoolmaster and the priest to come, too."

Farlik, the master butcher, arrived and exclaimed over the forester's skill at the butcher's art. "Now," he said, "I'll have less work to do. Not many pigs are lucky enough to die this way. This one died a hero's death in honor and glory, as the newspapers used to say during the war."

The water in the kettle was already boiling, the wooden washtub stood ready, and the master butcher prepared the pitch that would pull off the pig's bristles and leave the skin clean. With the help of the women, he set to work.

When the steamed pig was laid out, deathly white as a sheet, the forester shuffled shamefacedly into the kitchen. He greeted Farlik, offered him some snuff, and said resignedly, "A week more or less, it makes no difference. Now it's dead, we just start sooner. The aim was good and the death painless."

"Aye, painless," agreed Farlik, "and heroic, too."

"I'm still a good shot, dog damn it," grunted the forester.

88

Grandson Pepik, of course, was the one most pleased by the unexpected feast. Not even a cannibal child sitting down to feast on his own grandfather could have been more pleased. Pepik got into everything, no use trying to keep him out, and Catcher was even worse. Forgetting his pain, the dachshund hobbled around the kitchen and never took his eyes off the butcher. This was Catcher's idea of a feast, and when he got near to the cold, gutted pig, he planted a grateful kiss on its snout.

"That Sharp-Ears isn't so crazy after all!" he thought. And the rooster, an inexperienced youngster with whom Catcher could never strike up the kind of friendship he'd had with his predecessors, insolently threatened to tell on him.

Eventually the distinguished guests insisted that the butcher Farlik join them at the table. The feast was like a wedding banquet: pig's head, hog jowls, milt, liver, lungs, heart, ears, and—oh, best of all—the pig's snout.

"Delicious!" exclaimed the forester, smacking his lips.

Poor Catcher tried to stretch himself up to the edge of the kettle and wished he had at least two more noses to smell all the wonderful smells. Saliva drooled from his excited mouth.

Pepik, who never could get enough of anything, had stuffed his own stomach and was sitting there huffing and puffing like a fat goose, now and then throwing Catcher a bit of crackling or a piece of sausage.

The dining room bulged with food, drink, smoke, talk, jokes, hilarity. The group's merriment wasn't quite so noisy and unbridled as it would have been in Pasek's tavern, because here at home women's ears had to be respected. On the other hand, it was a good opportunity for wise conversation, though from the very start the priest tried to get the forester and the schoolmaster into an argument.

"I don't do much shooting," said the schoolmaster, to whom

89

the butcher had whispered the reason for the surprise pig feast, "but I should think that to kill a pig you would need a powerful shot."

"Well, that all depends on what kind of pig it is," answered the forester. "If it's a young, inexperienced one, even a fading moon will knock it down."

The priest caught the forester's meaning. Neighbor Fric, the bricklayers' foreman, had confessed to him after that infamous September Sunday card party at Pasek's, the one that ended so drunkenly, that he himself had sinned by failing to admonish a sinning neighbor. Then he had described in detail the schoolmaster's adventure with the sunflowers, which the country folk sometimes call "moons."

"Last night," the priest said, aiming barbs at both his friends, "the moon must have been pretty strong. Who knows? Maybe that was what knocked the pig down."

The forester got the point and remembered his bath of the preceding night. Not finding the memory very funny, he hastily changed the subject. "Gentlemen!" he pontificated, "you are all bachelors by choice, the Reverend Father here also out of duty. Until now I have always told you, 'Don't get married! Enjoy your freedom!' But now I say, 'Get married, and do it soon.' An unmarried man is like an animal: only when tied in some way can he shed his wildness. Take, for example, our fox. Last night did not see the last of her tricks. There will be more, I'm sure. All because she is free. No knot has tied her. Wait! You're laughing at me, and I don't blame you. Keep on laughing. But I've said it before and I'll say it again: even her time to go crazy will come. I'll still be here to see it! And then—"

"And then," Farlik grunted through his cigar, "we'll all have another pig feast!"

And so they all began to talk about the good old days, about love, about youthful escapades. The beer dwindled and the night increased, and soon it was coming close to midnight, time to get up and go home. Farlik would have loved to see Anna once more, but he felt his tongue and legs were no longer reliable.

"But she's really something," he said aloud. "Just right. Just the right height, just the right width!"

And the pining schoolmaster thought of his aging ideal, Miss Terynka, and with a sigh said that unfortunately it is not only sunflowers that ripen and fade.

The priest said nothing.

After their goodbyes, they all began the journey home. The night sky was dark and moonless, snow hung in the air, and walking through the woods was like walking on eiderdown, though they occasionally stumbled over the crooked roots that spidered weblike over their path.

"Gentlemen, it would be a shame if one of us was to fall," said Farlik wisely. "It is better that we all fall together. I'm used to leading two oxen with one hand. Hold on to me."

They all linked arms, and sure enough, the journey did seem to go faster.

That same night Sharp-Ears sat behind the juniper bushes, pondering her difficult situation. It was impossible to think, for the ruthless grumbling of her stomach drowned her thoughts. Resorting to the classic student remedy, she pushed her paws against her stomach and promised her belly it would have a grand time at the first opportunity.

All of a sudden she heard human voices along the path to the glen. Her first impulse was to flee, but then she realized she was safe. The voices could not belong to hunters because they were neither cursing nor boasting. The vixen listened carefully: no doubt about it, these men were coming from the forester's house.

"Hold on," she thought. "Now I can find out what's been happening there after last night." She listened attentively, but though she could hear every word of their conversation, most of it made no sense.

"That Anna," the butcher was saying, "is some fine girl. Flesh like goose down, plump as a pillow. Even St. Florian with his bucket would have a hard time putting out the fire she kindles in a man. Broad and tall like a fir tree, fetlocks set nice and low . . ."

"What does that mean, 'fetlocks set nice and low'?" asked the schoolmaster.

"That's what we say about horses. It means her legs are good, the ankles set just right, nice and low."

"I think these grapes are too high," said the priest in a fatherly tone.

"No matter. Let them be high. What's too high can be reached with a ladder," replied the butcher, unperturbed. "I'd take that bit of livestock without even bargaining for it. And you, schoolmaster, what do you think? You are going to get crazy like me, I think."

"Well, maybe later," said the schoolmaster longingly. "What's not ripe in the autumn may be ripe in the spring."

"It's amazing what one pig can do to some people," the priest said with a laugh.

"Please, Reverend Father!" protested the butcher. "We don't need a pig to think this way. It's not written that we all have to die bachelors!"

The company passed by, leaving the vixen perplexed and disappointed that her spying had spied out so little. She shook her bushy tail angrily and was about to head for home when her nose caught a whiff of something interesting. The men had been given party food to take home, as is the custom, and the aroma trailed tantalizingly behind them.

"That's odd. There must have been a feast at the human den. If that's true, the whole house will be sleeping it off. I may as well go have a look."

Soon she was creeping up to the forester's house. Everything was quiet, even Catcher. "He must have stuffed himself good. Now he's snoring, that pig of a dog."

Smoke was still pouring from the chimney, and the house was wreathed in fragrant smells. Everything tempted Sharp-Ears to have a look inside.

"Mmmm, would I love to have something to eat," she thought hungrily.

She would have sped to the house like an arrow, but something made her hesitate: every window was lit so brightly it hurt her eyes. By now the smoke from the chimney was thinning out and trailing down like a limp banner, but the house seemed to be awake. She could not know there was no reason to worry. The light in Anna's room was merely a signal for gamekeeper Spacek to come and tap at her window, the kitchen was lit because the forester's wife was making a cup of strong coffee for her husband, and the light in the bedroom was burning because poor Pepik was sick to his stomach. Even the greedy Catcher had taken advantage of the after-party confusion by crawling under the kitchen stove, happy that for once he did not have to sleep in the cold doghouse in the courtyard.

For a moment the vixen stood undecided, her body taut as a fiddle string. Then she tossed her head and silently ran toward the house as fast as the wind, no longer able to resist. "I'll just sneak in where the lights aren't on," she thought.

In a corner behind the house stood a stack of logs. She jumped to the top, and a heavenly smell streamed out of the little window and struck her right on the nose. Stretching her neck, she peered inside just as she once had peered into the badger's palace and— Oh, my God! Look what's here!—the pantry was stuffed with meat! Sausages were everywhere, packed on the shelves like fish eggs!

There was no time for the vixen to use her head: her empty belly drove her instantly forward. With one jump she was inside the pantry, and with another she had knocked down the sausages. They rolled to the floor, white and fragrant and soft as a maiden's elbows. Sharp-Ears sank her teeth into one and her tail went numb with ecstasy.

"Only the devil knows why humans sometimes eat such beastly food, when other times they can make a feast worthy of the house of God in His heavenly kingdom!"

She stuffed herself to the point of bursting, her belly stretching and bulging, until she finally had to stop to breathe. By that time she was so thirsty that her tongue felt stiff as a piece of wood. She cast a last satisfied look around the pantry and selected two more sausages, not quite so spicy, to take along on her journey home, then turned toward the window.

She had a hard time trying to jump back up. Carefully she climbed up the fallen shelf board, using it as a gangplank, and finally reached the window. Sated by all the delicacies, she didn't care that on her way out she was knocking most of the leftover sausages to the floor. Finally she sneaked away from the house— by now it had grown dark and quiet—and set out for her den.

She slept badly. Her stomach churned and protested all night, and she had to run out every few minutes to lap icicles off a small fir tree.

The forester, though, slept like a log. In the morning he got up singing, slung his rifle over his shoulder, and hurried into the forest to check on his workers, who were cutting trees not far away. On the way, he stopped at the log-collecting station and was surprised to find his colleague Spacek so sleepy.

"Listen, Spacek, come by the house this afternoon," he said, thinking of the slivovitz and the sausages. "You didn't get much sleep, and I've got something in my house that will fix you up."

"I know you do," Spacek said with a grin, thinking of what the forester had in his house that had kept him awake most of the night. But he didn't feel he should explain in detail, and the forester didn't seem interested in hearing, for he already had turned on his heel and within a minute was descending the hill toward his house. When he got to the farmyard, he fished his knife out of his pocket, hung his rifle in the hallway, opened the knife, and headed straight for the pantry.

At the sight of the pantry, the knife fell from his hand. His knees shook and he stared thunderstruck at his beloved sausages strewn over the floor like strangled chickens.

"Who did this?" he roared. In the kitchen, his wife turned to stone at the sound of his voice.

"Dog damn it! That blasted Pepik!" stormed the forester. "Why do you let him tear up things like a marten?"

"For God's sake, Pepik's been sick in bed ever since last night. The poor child can't stand the sight of food! And there you go, blaming him!"

"But just look in there!" wailed the forester. "Who else could have made all this mess?"

The wife was just as stunned as her husband. But with the sharp eye of a woman, she examined the scene of disaster and burst out, "Didn't I keep telling you, old man, close that window? But no! You never would! Everything would go bad, you said. Go bad when it's freezing?! Now you've gone and done it! That wretch of a fox must have sniffed out the pig feast and invited herself in!"

96

In its whole life the little pantry had never heard such swearing—it wasn't nearly big enough to hold all the names Bartos called Sharp-Ears or all the curses he called down on her head.

When he finally ran out of breath, he helped his wife pick up everything from the floor and arrange the sausages in neat rows again. But his work in the pantry was not yet over. He went out and came back with a rock and some rope.

"What are you trying to do now?" asked the wife.

"Make a trap. I'll let her have some more sausages, and then you'll have a new muff. I'll get her this time or never. She'll come and she'll get caught."

"You know something, old man," said the wife bitterly, "getting some peace and quiet in this house would almost be worth a few sausages. But you'd better swear she won't do more damage."

"Don't you worry, any more damage would be our fault. I'll see to it she doesn't get out of here with her skin."

All day the forester kept checking his ingenious trap. At noon, before he sat down to a soup made of pig's blood and barley, he got up restlessly and went into the pantry again. There he looked at the rows of jars filled with the same blood soup, dark as sweet sin and greasy as a butcher's shop.

"Who cares what else she ate," he said as if reciting a prayer of thanks, "as long as she left the soup alone."

The crocks of headcheese, the marinated meat for smoked sausages, the fillets smooth as a baby's cheek—everything was intact. The forester counted his riches again and again, dreaming of future feasts, tasting them all in his mind.

In her den, Sharp-Ears was tasting them, too. No longer afraid, certain of no danger, she set out early. The moon was glowing down through the clouds and onto the tops of firs and pines, the wind was singing gently in the branches, sleigh bells were tinkling somewhere in the distance as Sharp-Ears sprinted gracefully across the glassy blue snow.

As she ran boldly across a clearing that on more cautious nights she would have skirted, a hare darted in front of her. He had just awakened from a deep sleep and now stood staring stupidly at her. She was about to jump at him when she realized he was an old, lame grandfather, so she just gave him a sharp-tongued remark for crossing her path and bringing her bad luck.

"Next time, cover up your cotton tail, please! A dog two days dead would catch you standing there like that!"

"Stupid loudmouth!" shouted the hare, and he hid in the bushes to avoid a quarrel that might rouse the whole countryside.

The gable of the forester's house could now be glimpsed among the trees. Tonight the house stood quiet and dark, with only one faint light flickering in a small window.

"They're still sleeping off the feast," rejoiced Sharp-Ears, and with a jump reached the woodpile under the pantry window. Perhaps she was tired from running, or maybe the hare's appearance had upset her, but now she stopped and felt a twinge of fear. "Should I or shouldn't I?" she thought. "What if the house is dark and quiet on purpose, and they are waiting? People aren't that much more stupid than we are. Somehow I don't like all this."

Then she made a dismissive gesture with her paw and, as on the night before, jumped onto the woodpile and into the pantry. A suspicious click followed, but Sharp-Ears paid no attention. After all, the white sausages were lying there in nice rows again, the blood sausages meticulously coiled as before. The sight made her jaws ache to bite them.

"I won't stay long," she promised herself. "God only knows what might happen." She turned straight to the shelf with the blood sausages, grabbed the fattest one, and gleefully headed for the window.

99

She could not believe her eyes. The window was shut. She felt cold all over, the hairs on her back stood on end, and she almost whimpered aloud. Her appetite and her courage vanished. She sat down in a corner, clasped her paws prayerfully, and tried to think. The longer she thought, the more frightened she became. She stared desperately at the window, hoping it would open, but no, it would not. The window stayed shut.

She saw clearly that she had got herself into a trap. She dropped the sausage onto the floor, hung her head, and began to cry. So gentle was her crying, no human could cry that way. After relieving her sorrowing soul, she wiped away her tears, crouched far back into the corner to be better protected in case of attack, and thought of the past. She remembered the morning of the green frog's arrival at her parents' den, her abduction by the forester, her growing up in servitude, and how she had broken free. When her anguish reached its climax and she was at the brink of despair, her usual composure reasserted itself.

"Let him come!" she snarled furiously. "God knows I won't leave one thing standing in here. A fox can defend herself, and she will, too!"

Shuffling footsteps came from the hallway. The vixen sprang under the table. On top of it stood countless jars: gooseberry preserves, currant jelly, pickled tomatoes, eggs in brine, dill pickles, lingonberries, mushrooms, mustard, fish marinated in wine. The biggest jars were filled with the pig's-blood soup the forester loved so much—a joyful sight, a feast for the eyes. Sharp-Ears, though, cared for none of these things now.

Someone touched the door handle. The door squeaked faintly and, ever so slowly, began to open. A hand slipped inside, then a nose, and finally the familiar head, hat and beard included. The forester was peeking into the pantry. Sharp-Ears twitched nervously under the table, tempted to dash out and start her devil's dance immediately. She was deeply ashamed and embarrassed to have gone crazy and let herself be caught like this.

"Should I at least stick out my tongue at him?" she thought. "No, let him enjoy his fun, at least for the moment. If I don't get angry, he will—and everyone acts crazy as a cow when they get angry."

She shuffled her legs because they were beginning to cramp. Then she yawned softly.

"Dog damn it!" exclaimed the forester. "She's here!"

He slammed the door shut and left. His malicious voice and the sound of hurried movements could be heard through the door. "I see, he's calling the family to come watch him beat Sharp-Ears!" The vixen stretched her limbs and hurriedly combed her fur to prove she was not upset. Then she resigned herself again to dull waiting.

After gathering the family, the forester entered the gun room, trailed by the entire household—except Anna, who was scared of all weapons but Spacek's. On the wall hung firearms of the Lancaster and Lefaucheux types, rifles, fowling pieces, revolvers, cartridge boxes, a spyglass, and a few heavy clubs—such an armory that the forester was at a loss as to which weapon to choose. He finally reached for a rifle, but Celestyn, his helper, stopped him.

"You're going to shoot indoors?" he said ironically.

"What do you mean, indoors? You want me to chase her over the manure pile?" roared the forester. "I don't want to drown myself again!"

He looked down the gun barrel, which glistened like the eye of a snake. He tested the triggers, pleased with their smooth action. The decision made, he loaded the rifle, but was stopped by his wife, who had practical reasons for interfering.

"You're not going hunting in the pantry!" snapped his wife. "You'll break the windows! You might shoot somebody outside! Get a club and beat her up!"

"A club and a beating," declared the forester, "won't teach any vixen a lesson. That's like a farmer I heard about, he used a flail to punish his wife. But he'd sooner have threshed a shock of rye sheaves—half dead and she'd still talk back. A vixen is no different."

"So do what you like," sighed his wife. "But let me tell you, old man, you've always been hard as quartz. Look there at those leashes. Remember what you used them for? You put your own children on a leash when they were little so they wouldn't run all over the woods. You only cared about your pipe and your own comfort, and you kept the poor little things leashed like dogs."

The reproach cut the forester to the quick. It was true. He had indeed put the children on leashes when they begged him to take them into the woods. But that was because he knew he was absent-minded, and he worried about forgetting them somewhere, and so the children trotted before him on the leashes like hounds. It had been rather cruel.

He unloaded the rifle, hung it back on the wall, and picked up a club. But what a club! Made from a knotty plum tree, it was rugged, stiff, heavy, and dangerous. Pepik's mouth opened in amazement. For his own beatings, a switch was considered suffi-cient. In his heart he felt sorry for Sharp-Ears, whom he had not seen in such a long time.

"Grandpa, can I come with you?" he begged.

"Just to the door," his grandfather replied in a sharp voice. "You might get hit, too, and it would be hard to fetch a doctor this time of night."

Pepik did not insist. He was sure that today's beating would be worse than all the ones he had ever received since the day he was born, put together.

"Don't even ask me how I'm going to clobber her," boasted the forester. "When she's dead, I'll tear that greedy gullet out of her and you'll have a fur fit for a countess."

All this time, Sharp-Ears was crouching under the table. From the hall she could now hear a mumble of male and female voices, the stamping of heavy boots, and the clicking of women's heels. Pepik was talking—he sounded frightened—and Catcher was barking as if he were chasing away a beggar at lunchtime. That nuisance of a dog was the last thing she needed!

Again the door opened, but this time, instead of a hand, a club slipped in. Sharp-Ears could not restrain herself any longer. Grimacing, she bared her teeth and bristled all over. The forester crouched, raised the club, and slowly advanced on the vixen.

"Listen, old man! Let her be! Something awful's going to happen!" pleaded the wife, sticking her head in at the door.

"You be quiet now, woman! This is a man's job!" He aimed the club at the vixen but hit the table leg instead.

The bristling Sharp-Ears opened her mouth threateningly and snarled in fury. "Stop it! Don't push me!"

The forester interpreted her growls as a plea for mercy. He swung at her again and this time connected with her paw. At that moment, she decided to destroy the pantry. The blow had numbed her paw but not her spirit, which rebelled against the outrage. She stuck her head out from under the table and angrily barked at the forester.

"Aren't you ashamed, old grandpa, to torture an animal? First you trap me and then you come at me with a club! How would you like it if I tricked you into my den and beat you there? If you hit me once more, I'll come out to face you and then we'll see who will win. Are you so stingy you won't spare a scrap of food? You have plenty and I have nothing. I'm no beggar, I only came here and took a bit. Hit me again if you want, but let me tell you that you're going to have to go begging yourself!"

104 The forester stepped back to the door, and Sharp-Ears thought he had had a change of heart. She was wrong.

He swung the club and hit her on the nose, hard. Something cracked.

"Tyrant!" she hissed through her pain. The forester had no second chance to strike, for the vixen arched her back and bounded wildly onto the table. All the bottled treasures landed in a pile of rubble and ruin on the floor: cheese floated in thick soup, fish mixed with the jam, pickles rolled into headcheese; splintered glass crunched under the forester's uncertain feet, and with every step his boots sank into the dark, sticky mess on the floor.

"You asked for it!" screamed the vixen in a fury of anger, pain, and shame. "And I'm just getting started! I'm not going to leave you a drop for your greedy mouth!"

The club whizzed through the air, the forester panted and swore, and the vixen slithered this way and that like a serpent. The pantry erupted into a battlefield of groans, crashes, kicks, dull blows, and sharp smells. Sauerkraut spilled out of the barrel; the beer keg lost its bottom and drowned all the sausages; demijohns of juniper and plum brandies shattered. Nothing stayed where it was—even the two fine smoked hams went sailing, describing a circle above the scene as if tossed by superbly skilled circus jugglers.

The forester's eyes saw nothing except the vixen's rust-red back, and his ears heard nothing but her angry barking, egging him on. Mushrooms turned into gravy under his feet, his soles smeared the floor tiles with mustard, his heels crushed jars and bottles into glass slivers. Brine splashed everywhere. It looked as if the Last Judgment had arrived—the only thing missing was trumpet fanfares.

The forester hit Sharp-Ears's back. Crouching to absorb the shock, she hurled a piece of blood sausage in his face. He swung again and this time knocked down a shelf housing aged round

105

cheeses, golden and runny, thin and shapeless with time like old men. Sharp-Ears was leaping through the air from one corner to another. The greater the chaos, the wider the pantry door opened. The wife, horrified by the terrible scene, tried vainly to calm her husband and glared daggers at Celestyn, who was standing there like a tree trunk.

"Maybe he *should* have brought the gun!" she reproached herself. Pepik decided that definitely the best viewing point for such a wild chase was from below. First he sat down, then got onto his knees, and finally lay flat on the threshold, eyes bulging like snail stalks. At long last the desperate Sharp-Ears noticed the audience and the open door and saw salvation at hand.

"Out of here and away!"

To the forester's surprise, she ducked behind a pile of rubble and, using the table and shelves for cover, bared her teeth and addressed him. "Monster!" she barked at the top of her voice. "One more blow and I'll jump you! I'm not afraid of you even if you *are* twice my size!"

Foolishly, the forester decided that it was now time for a final attack. Flushed and breathing hard, he crept on tiptoe toward her. His feet were slipping and sliding, meat gravy squished in his boots, but he didn't care. "Now you'll get it right across the head!" he threatened Sharp-Ears.

"Or *you* will!" she shrieked furiously.

Suddenly Sharp-Ears's front paw parted his hair, her tail whacked him on the nose, and with one powerful leap she was over him and through the door. There she paused to catch her breath and calmly looked back at the forester.

He had lost his balance. Reeling, staggering like an undercut tree, he dropped the club and fell heavily to the floor, landing in the repulsive slime, on top of a mashed slab of cheese. He tried to stand up and reach for his club again to punish Sharp-Ears for her unexpected trickery, but he was stuck to the floor like a sparrow in birdlime. The gooey sludge was seeping through his pants and into his pockets, and he had hit the floor so hard that he wasn't sure if he was in one piece or not.

"Mother! Please! Help me up!" he begged pitifully. "I'm going to drown in this mess! It's thick as the Dead Sea and I can't get out of it! Dog damn it!"

Alarmed by the sudden calm in the pantry, through which the forester's voice sounded as if from an abyss, the wife pushed open the door and stared in disbelief.

It was then that Sharp-Ears, seeing neither point nor profit in staying any longer, declared to herself: "There's nothing more for me here. Catcher can lick up what's behind me, if he wants."

Waving her tail in heroic triumph, Sharp-Ears
ran toward the front door. The hallway was
dark, but outside the sparkling snow lit up
the night and the full moon shone in the early-
morning sky like a giant fish eye. Sharp-Ears, though, had no
time to look around and sped through the house recklessly,
knocking down and hurling aside anything blocking her way.
Pepik's legs came first; using teeth and claws, she roughly pushed
them away, and Pepik, screaming with fear, grabbed on to his
grandmother, pulling her down with him as she in turn pulled
down the forester's helper. With a resolute leap, Sharp-Ears sailed
over the pile of human bodies, regretting only that she was in
a hurry and could not play them some foxy trick. Remembering
what she had done to evict the badger, she wished she had the
time to do the same thing to these humans for today's beating.

By now the chase in the pantry, the stamping feet, the screams,
and the blows had aroused the whole place. Even the hens were
up, cackling with curiosity and crowding around the front door.

They had unanimously agreed that this time the fox would not come out alive and were telling each other what a relief that would be. The young rooster, inexperienced and boastful, ruffled up his feathers, crowed, and stood on his toes so as not to miss a single detail of the performance.

"I'll give you something to look at!" growled the vixen and flashed her teeth at him.

The rooster suspected a major change in the course of history, because screaming and sounds of the utmost confusion were still coming from inside the house. It sounded precisely as if a skunk were visiting the chicken coop. The rooster shifted from one leg to the other, squawking a retreat, and ran for cover under the wheelbarrow. The hens began cackling and Catcher, back in the house, began to bark, while in the garden behind the fence the two hunting dogs were carrying on as if they'd lost their minds. Anna was screaming hysterically in her attic room, afraid to come downstairs, perhaps because she was not alone.

In one word, it was a madhouse. Only old Whisker the tomcat continued his unperturbed stroll along the ridge of the roof between the chimney and the weathervane, his groomed fur and combed mustache confirming that he was on his way to a rendezvous. Setting his paws down in a noble manner, as befits a well-bred creature, he meowed impatiently while making sure his tail was held graceful and straight as a candle, in strict adherence to the rules of feline manners.

"You're the only sensible creature around here!" Sharp-Ears called up to him as she reached the other side of the courtyard. The cold winter air had cleared her head, and she realized that her bottom was burning and itching from the vinegar and pepper splashed all over the pantry. She raised her tail, shook out her

109

rumpled fur—like a girl who is about to sit in a church pew and doesn't want to crease her skirts—and plopped herself down in the snow. The icy compress felt good. Her mind had calmed, and she was beginning to feel hungry after the hectic chase.

"God Eternal, to think what waste we caused with our dance, the forester and me!" she thought. "Now he's got what he asked for. His stomach will soon be grumbling, too."

But the forester's stomach did not grumble when he got out of the sticky mess he had been sitting in. He rubbed his eyes and clutched his head at the sight of the destruction he had caused. His wife, not yet recovered from her fright, had joined him in the pantry and was equally dazed. Grandson Pepik was afraid to open his mouth, but the forester's helper clasped his hands behind his back and summed up the situation in a short but profound speech.

"That's that," he intoned judiciously.

"Well," said the forester limply, "it looks like we made a mess. Why didn't I shoot the beast? I couldn't possibly have done as much damage as she did. Bread here, eggs there, jars all smashed. Dear God, just look at this man-made mess, if you can."

But lamenting did not help. The ham snuggled in the plum jam, tomatoes bobbed in the blood soup, sausages swam in spilled mustard. Catcher, who somehow had got out of the kitchen, looked fearfully at what the humans had wrought.

"It's not so bad," he thought. "Humans are so picky and fussy that they'll leave it all for me."

While the people were wailing in the pantry, a new chase had begun in the courtyard. It was a determined one, but shorter and more profitable. Sharp-Ears had caught the rooster.

"Now out of here quickly, before the old man pulls himself

together," she growled, gently holding her victim's neck in her jaws. She sped toward the woods, a triumphant smile on her face, pleased at having done a good deed. For a short moment the rooster flapped his wings and complained while Sharp-Ears soothed him with tender words.

111

"Never mind, dear little rooster, that I'm going to wring your neck. Your people do it, too, but their ways are worse, for they wring each other's neck all the time. Your picture used to symbolize freedom and revolution, but now the rooster has grown fat and learned to act like a lord, shouting all over the courtyard. And so, with a nice snap, you'll make room for a new one. As for your flock, don't you cry for them—they'll get used to a new rooster pretty fast."

The forest murmured deeply and gloomed darker than night itself. The snow was turning soft; a warm spell was coming. The vixen felt free. She had forgotten the club, the trap, the human cruelty. Cheerfully and with good appetite, she tore into the poor rooster. Then, sated, she sat down comfortably at her doorway and for a long, long time pondered humans, their troubles, and their weaknesses.

"They are a worse mob than the forest animals, and they call us unreasoning and wild. We devour only animals of other species, not our own kind, but look what the human animal does! How glad I am that I'm not a dumb creature like man, that I have four legs and the gifts of reason and free will. Let man play the master. Soon he'll kill the last of his kind and destroy his race. We foxes are on the rise; we'll rise above man and the time will come when we'll gobble up the last human cub, just like I did that stupid rooster tonight.

"I smile and I laugh and I sing because spring is coming. Already it's wandering somewhere behind these woods and looking for the path to us. This year I'll be older and wiser. Just watch how I'll go after the forester and all his kind. Who knows, perhaps I'll become the liberator of the entire animal race! Who else can devour the forest like me, the ever-hungry Sharp-Ears?"

Shrovetide weather set in. Everything began to thaw. The forest seemed suddenly darker, every twig sharply outlined against the white background of snow; a breath of soft, fragrant air ascended from the glens and valleys; larger and larger bare spots, warmed by the sun, appeared on the slopes. Clear drops rolled off branches and poured down in denser and denser showers, rainbows in their tiny droplets, a sweet springtime song.

Joyful sounds and jubilant songs resounded in the treetops, and even the most ancient pine trees were moved. The sun no longer hurried to bed as in the winter, but stayed, lingering, as if it could not feast its eyes long enough on an earth so worthy of kisses, of love, of tender caresses. Hazelnut bushes glowed with the gold of their catkins, and tiny purple flowers bloomed longingly, like the lips of a maiden eager to become the lips of a woman, loving and loved.

At noontime on this lovely sunny day, Sharp-Ears woke earlier than usual and sprawled her body comfortably at the entrance of her den. A strange and unidentifiable emotion had taken hold of her. She felt like laughing and crying and, at the same time, somewhat cross. Never before in all her life had she felt like this. And when the southern wind, the one always followed within three days by rainy weather, started to blow, it brought to her a very distant echo of music. In the village beyond the forest, a band was gaily playing at a village dance.

"Horrible animals, those humans," said Sharp-Ears, and yawned. "I don't understand them. One moment they're sulky as devils, and the next they're hopping around like wagtails."

She fell silent as the sound of heavy footsteps reached her from beneath the slope. "What has the devil brought now?" she grumbled, and pricked up her ears. The footsteps were coming closer, a resolute sniffle was heard, and a red handkerchief appeared on the path. A man was wiping his forehead and nose with it. He stopped, took a deep breath, and began to sing an old folk song:

> *While I was out a-roaming,*
> *I heard the band a-drumming,*
> *And I found my sweetheart*
> *At her window, humming.*

"He hollers as if he were in his own back yard," muttered the vixen, and examined the man with curiosity. He looked like any other man, but his Austrian army cap was new to her. Even more noteworthy was the load he was carrying on his back in a wicker hamper. It contained several ducks and hens who, agog with curiosity, were observing the world around them. Sharp-Ears jumped up as if she'd been stung by a wasp.

114

"I should test you and see what sort of man you are!" she thought. She waited until the man with the hamper passed by, then she ran swiftly and took a shortcut to cross the path directly in front of him. Skipping and limping, she dragged her hindquarters clumsily behind her, as if unable to use them.

The trick worked. The man came out of the bend in the path and spotted the vixen. He rubbed his eyes, for he never before had seen a fox in broad daylight like this. It has to be explained that a citizen of Lisen and a fox are natural enemies, for they both live on poultry. If a Lisen citizen had four legs and a tail, he would be the fox's equal, because his nose is sharp and he can sniff out poultry anywhere.

"If I tell this to my old woman at home, she'll ask right away: 'How many did you have, Hypolit?' She'll never believe me, that a fox wouldn't run away from a Lisen citizen."

Hypolit Harasta, seller of butter, eggs, and poultry, stopped and reflected. "I couldn't be drunk. One, two, three tumblers of brandy, a couple of rye, that's not much for me."

His thoughts were completely clear, unclouded as the sky above. In his mind, he could distinctly picture his house in Lisen, and he could clearly imagine his wife in all her eloquence and all her horror.

"And I won't be allowed to answer one word. Doesn't she stir up the whole marketplace from end to end whenever the mood hits her? The commissioners, the policemen, me, everybody's afraid of her, and she's not afraid of anybody, not even the party. When we were protesting the high prices last year and smashed up all those shops, didn't she tell that comrade, the one who's the mayor now: 'Shut your big mouth and get out of here!'? And didn't she tell the rest of us standing around there:

'Go home, you beggars, you dirty tramps!'? I shivered with joy hearing her talk. Has anybody got such a strong-minded wife as my Apolena? And to a woman like that I should say on this day: 'Polinka, just imagine, I saw a fox in the middle of the road!' Won't she smash me one? Won't she start screaming that I'm trying to make a fool of her—her, my own wife and the good mother of seven? I'd better say nothing and just chase that fox a bit. If I catch her, then I can boast. So, Hypolit, put down the hamper and get a stick and follow her!"

There is no shortage of sticks in the woods. Hypolit Harasta broke off a big knotty branch and ran after the fox. The ducks, when they saw him, stretched their necks and quacked merrily at the spectacle. Harasta knew they were laughing at him, and the thought only egged him on to run faster.

"Just go on laughing," he said furiously, and did not look back at the hamper anymore.

At first, running was easy. The path was even, not packed down too much, but after a few meters it changed. If you have ever walked from Babice to Habruvka in the winter, you will remember what the path is like: all of a sudden it decides to slant down like the side of a roof, then goes along a level part all studded with sharp, pointed stones; then it abruptly shoots uphill and drops sharply downhill. Hypolit Harasta, strong as he was, got so tired after a while that he gladly would have turned back, but the fox seemed to falter, so he ignored his fatigue and kept up the pursuit. Sharp-Ears kept hopping and limping, carrying her tail in the careless fashion of a dressed-up shopkeeper's assistant carrying a cane on a Sunday outing, and ceaselessly racked her brain for some mischief she could do to the Lisen merchant.

"Aha, this should do it!" She grinned and turned down a steep slope into the glen. The path here was miserable, seldom used, cluttered with stones and stumps at every step—not long ago, Sharp-Ears had hurt the big toe of her right front paw here. She didn't quite believe that the lazy human would have the courage to follow her, but Hypolit Harasta's blood was boiling and he wouldn't have stopped for anything in the world. His feet slipped and his cap flew off his head, but he picked it up and scrambled on, hanging on to trees and shrubs to avoid falling down and to get across the icy mirrors of puddles. By now he was angry and his blood boiled even harder. He had stopped threatening and cursing and just tried to clutch his club as tightly as he could. Sharp-Ears would let him get so close that her bushy tail could tickle his face, then quickly jump away to avoid a blow.

And now, finally, what she had secretly been looking forward to happened. The hobnails clicked, the club whizzed off, the cap circled above the head, and Hypolit Harasta was in a heap, legs up and nose down. At full speed, the nose hit the stump that had hurt Sharp-Ears's big toe and was flattened like a red-hot nail between hammer and anvil. That terrible moment was barely a split second, but Harasta saw stars, and all the bones in his body rattled like a stack of kindling wood falling apart.

Getting up was not easy. The first thing he saw as he came to was the vixen's red tail and what gleamed beneath it. Sharp-Ears was no longer running but seemed to be floating like a maple leaf in the autumn air, grinning with satisfaction: "Now you take care of your nose, and I'll go take care of your hamper!"

Hypolit Harasta finally got up, but his legs were shaking and his body ached—in the back, the shoulders, everywhere. He felt as if he had lost his original shape and been mashed flat as a pancake. He felt all over his body to make sure he was still in

117

one piece and not just a rosary of ruins strung on what used to be Hypolit Harasta. Something terrible was happening with his nose, but his fingers were unable to locate that organ: instead, in the middle of his face was a soft, bloody, shapeless form that closely resembled a raw steak. It could be turned, at the cost of dreadful pain, to the right and to the left. The accident had not decreased its bulk—on the contrary, it was growing and swelling like a bud.

"For Christ's sake, what will I say to my wife when I see her! She'll think I've been in a fight! No matter what I swear by, she'll yell, 'You've been fighting!' and she won't let me say another word. That damned beast of a fox! Satan himself sent her my way."

It took a lot of effort to reassure himself that he really was the former Hypolit Harasta, and that this catastrophe of a nose really was his own. His knees hurt, his trousers were ripped, and his militant mood was totally gone.

While he suffered, Sharp-Ears rejoiced. Leaving the unfortunate merchant, she raced through the underbrush toward the spot where the hamper still lay. She jumped over roots, rocks, and washed-out ravines, shouting for joy at having duped a human, one slightly more cunning than the old forester.

"Look at him," she said delightedly. "He wanted to beat me for no reason, just because I'm a fox! Humans are strange. When I take a chicken, they fuss and cry, but here's a man carrying so many ducks he can't even count them all. And I shouldn't take one? He can't eat them all by himself, and here he breaks his back to drag them along. Every animal cares just for himself, so why doesn't every man care just for himself and his family? Why care for others? I can't understand it. Just you wait, you'll be surprised to see what I'll do to you, you profiteer!"

The ducks quacked in anguish when they saw the vixen. They knew all too well that their hour had come. Huddling together, lowering their necks, they bravely awaited their fate. Sharp-Ears wasted no time. She knocked over the hamper, spilled out the ducks and some eggs, and set to work at her hangman's task, an occupation at which she had long been a master. As she grabbed each duck's neck, there was a crack and her victim flapped its

119

wings, quacked for the last time, turned its eyes to the sky, and died. Sharp-Ears killed the first one with relish, but all of a sudden she was overcome with strange and unprecedented thoughts, with ideas that struck her as inappropriate for a fox.

"I know why people take care of others besides themselves! They love one another!" Thus reflecting, she resumed killing one duck after another, ending up with more than she needed, just like humans.

"They love one another!" she mused. "And I don't know what it is to love someone! With Catcher, it was childish play. I could hardly have fallen in love with the badger, because he had such a big belly and was so ridiculous, just like all other badgers. And so far, no one else has come my way. Oh, what an unhappy Vixen Sharp-Ears am I!"

By the time she had finished off all the ducks, her eyes were wet and her heart was filled with sorrow. The spring is coming and the vixen has no one to love. Oh, Autumn—sad, lonely, how beautiful you are, so much more beautiful than the spring! No strange, confused thoughts steal into the soul of a fox—there is no time for them because one's fur is molting. But mezereon soon will blossom, snowdrops and hellebores will appear, thrushes will sing and blackbirds call. Everyone will be happy, only Sharp-Ears will be alone, alone with her empty heart.

She shook her head but could not shake the lonely thoughts out of it; they plagued her worse than fleas. Hadn't she seen gamekeeper Spacek with Anna near the forester's house just the other day? They were standing under a larch tree, sighing and whispering, muzzle to muzzle, arms around each other's waist, walking around in a circle until they had paved a path in the snow.

"I'll leave what's human to humans. Maybe man is smarter,

but let me just be a fox," she thought. And sorrow such as she had never before experienced breathed on her through her thick winter pelt, which soon would thin and let the sorrow move even closer to her skin like a northern wind. She left her booty lying there and, deeply dejected, turned toward home.

Meanwhile, Hypolit Harasta had pulled himself together and, slowly, one foot before the other, was returning to his hamper. Now he stood silently looking at it, stunned, wringing his hands. His hair stood on end. He was speechless.

He had been picturing himself taking a fox skin home to his wife. And now this. The eggs all in a mess, the ducks slaughtered. Pulling out a handkerchief, Harasta wept and wept. Sharp-Ears stopped under an old oak tree and listened to his weeping. For the first time in her life it occurred to her that someone else's sorrow can be greater than one's own.

"And I wonder why they chase me," she whispered, "when I behave like this."

She no longer was interested in the duck she held carefully in her teeth. Now it disgusted her.

"No one loves me." Weeping, she ran toward her den. For the first time in her life she envied the forester his ability to curse.

And the forester was certainly cursing. After the stormy night and the wild chase in the pantry, he had come down with the Spanish flu and could not get out of its claws. Finally, after weeks of staying indoors and shuffling irritably around the house and courtyard in his dressing gown, he was able to get out into the woods again. He felt happy, almost as happy as the faithful Catcher, who was wild with joy: he would not leave anything alone today. Racing and running about as if he had lost his mind, he barked at jackdaws, at empty nests, and even nipped at the pants legs of Martinek, the wandering migrant worker, who, now that winter jobs in the forest had ended, was visiting the local brick kilns and looking for a snug summer's nook. The forester, caught up in the general cheerfulness, stopped to talk with Martinek and, since he could now smoke his pipe again, pressed a gift into Martinek's hand: an old cigar, one that had been forgotten in his pocket for a year and by now was shabby as a willow branch in a fast creek.

"So, Martinek, how's everything?" asked the forester, curious about Martinek's answer.

"Oh, yah, all would be well if it were not for my pesky wife. But thanks to my golden new republic and the new divorce laws, I'm going to divorce her."

"How will you manage without a wife? Who'll do your wash?"

"Why should I worry about that? Who's doing it now? My shirts haven't felt the touch of woman's hands in years. I'll manage without my wife, I'll manage just fine. And anyhow, sir, I've found myself a better one. Her name is Julka, and this is what I'm taking to her to cheer her up. Look at it. How could she fail to love me?"

Martinek pulled a flat flask out of his breast pocket, shook it, held it up to the sun, looked lovingly at the golden bubbles bobbing inside, took a long swallow, then tenderly wiped the mouth of the flask on the palm of his hand and his own mouth on his sleeve.

"Aren't you poaching on my grounds, Martinek?" joked the forester.

"As sure as God is above me and the earth under my feet, no. Not by a single step. But I'm thinking about doing it," said Martinek seriously.

"Eh? What nonsense is that, you old sinner?"

"Well, you see, sir, the other day, here behind the clearing, I bumped into Harasta from Lisen, and I see he's busted his nose, sir, but really smashed it to bits and pieces, like a mashed potato. 'Who's fixed you up?' I says. 'Don't even ask me,' he says. 'A fox. You have'—so he says—'a bad forester. He sits at home like a potbellied stove while the forest crawls with foxes. If he doesn't shoot them, then we will. We'll shoot everything in sight!' 'How

123

come?' I says. 'You mean a fox busted up your nose?' 'Well, it was like this,' he says. 'She pretends to limp, I go after her, stumble a little over some stump, and my nose turns into a mashed potato.' So I says to myself, 'You got drunk, you stumbled over your own hangover, and now you want to blame it on the fox and the forester. You big liar, it serves you right. You ought to stay sober like I do.' "

"That's right, dog damn it," the forester grimly agreed.

"But no, sir, I saw with my own eyes that what he said was the truth."

"You're drunk, too."

"Not very much, sir, oh no, except for a sip or two. I just saw the fox a few steps from here, and within a stone's throw there's a dead hare. I wanted to pick it up, but lucky for me, something inside me said, 'Leave it, you'll get yourself in trouble.' "

The forester said no more, straightened the rifle on his shoulder, and headed for the clearing, Catcher in tow.

Martinek was right. At the edge of the clearing, under a dry pine tree, lay a hare, completely dead, long cold, and near it were the tracks of a fox. Catcher, without even touching the hare, began expertly sniffing the spoor. Obviously it was one familiar to him.

"May lightning strike her! It was Sharp-Ears, dog damn it. She'll never stop making trouble."

And somewhere, far in the distance beyond the forest, church bells began to ring the noon hour. The sky shone clear and blue, and the sound of the bells vibrated clearly, like tiny blue butterflies over sun-drenched meadows on a summer day. Spring indeed was coming back, pausing somewhere near a warm ocean and waiting for migratory birds to gather for their journey north, toward our region. The forester vividly imagined the arrival of the house martins, how they would warm their nests again and cheer the courtyard with their chattering sounds, how the barn swallows would flit over the roof, how the forest soon would resound with the many-voiced song.

The old man rejoiced.

"Ah well, so be it, the twilight of my life. I still am glad when toward evening time the sun glistens. When my time comes, it will beckon me with its finger, and together we will lie down to sleep."

Turning to Catcher, he began talking to him, as was his old habit. "Don't just sit there staring like a good-for-nothing. We'll run home, leave off my stuff, get the trap, and you'll see what we'll fix up for her!"

Catcher wagged his tail as if to say, "Of course, as you wish, old sir."

In the afternoon, they set the trap for the fox—cautiously, slowly, cleverly. "She's bound to come back for that fat hare," said the forester. He spread the jaws of the trap, placed the hare on top of it, and in good spirits wandered off through the clearing.

How splendid stood the forest! On the branches, remnants of snow were melting and falling down in drops at times clear and pure, then rainbow-colored, then like silvery drops of liquefied light; and the unceasing, eternal, tender song in the treetops sounded alternately like weeping and laughter. Fragments of old fairy tales surfaced in the forester's mind, and unwittingly, he began weaving them into his own vague fable: Primeval nymphs are returning home to their ancient seats, greeting one another and weeping for joy, dancing delightedly in their white robes— and once again Maytime and love will come to them, and they will distribute the sweet dew of happiness into the blossoms of a million primroses and sweet peas and anemones, and people will come and walk in silence, their heads bowed, knowing that super-natural bliss is all around them, their feet wading in it as in the morning dew—and then the nymphs will leave again and go far, far away to other realms where their magic hands are needed, to help man forget his sorrows and return home to the embrace of the earth, the mother who nourishes us all.

The forester rubbed his forehead to chase away the vision, and smiled bitterly. "I'm getting childish, getting old. Dog damn it . . ."

He quickly left the warmth of the clearing and turned into a gloomy ravine. There it was still cold, icicles and frozen snow clinging to the branches. As evening drew on, the frost settled, and stars sprang one by one out of the blue depths of the sky until it seemed to be sprinkled with silver dust. The forest had grown silent, become as quiet as a lake locked in ice. Without realizing it, the forester had strolled full circle, back again to the clearing where, in the dusk, the hare was lying in the steel trap: it was a strangely sad sight, that dead head with its staring eyes—extin-guished lights.

Catcher realized that his master did not feel like talking. He did not bark, did not jump or play, but walked solemnly three steps in front of the forester, taking care to stay out of range of his walking stick. Saddened, the old man returned to his house. Warmed by the hot stove, comforted by the four walls, he slowly began to feel better.

Sharp-Ears, meanwhile, was beginning to stir. It was early in the evening and after the sleepless, wasted day, she had a headache and felt out of sorts. Reproaching herself for giving up her sleep for no reason, she decided to do penance. For a start, she cleaned her den until it looked so neat and comfortable that she felt no desire to leave it.

"I'll go out for a short run," she thought, "and come right back." But as she walked toward the juniper bushes, she decided differently.

It was a magical evening, mysterious as the depths of a river, the sky a bottomless blue abyss adorned with shimmering stars and a sliver of moon, the silhouettes of trees, bushes, everything as clear as if etched on metal. The air was a fountain of delight bursting like a cold spring from heavenly heights. Sharp-Ears knew she could not stay home on such a night. She ran over the hard-packed snowdrifts, detoured through the tall trees, and now and then brushed against the fragile icicles that the singing silver

127

water drops had formed, striking sounds from them like tiny elfin cimbaloms. She ran farther and farther until she approached the site of her morning adventures.

Rounding a bend in the path, she saw the dead hare. She sat down, looked at it for a while, and reflected: "Poor thing, look at it lying there. I killed it for no reason. But I'm tired of ducks and chickens, and a bit of hare meat might be nice."

The hare looked appetizing, but she immediately felt ashamed of herself and began scolding: "All I'm thinking about is my belly again, just like man. Can't I think of anything nobler? Why think of people and food all the time? Even now, when there's not a trace of humans, I think about them. They're so ugly, so repulsive. I'm glad foxes don't smell the way they do."

She decided to have a closer look at the hare and, as she bent down to it, noticed a spoor. It had a human smell.

"That's funny. Man was here and didn't take the hare. Is that possible? It's mine, I put it here, but he touched it with his hand and put it down again."

She carefully walked around the suspicious spot a few times. No doubt about it, man had set some trick here. But what? And who for?

"I know what it is!" She burst out laughing. "A steel trap! What does old Grandpa take me for? Does he think I'm some badger? Well, old man, you've got another think coming!" and she laughed until her belly ached. Examining the trap again, she sniffed the chain that held it to a small tree and laughed harder than ever.

"Isn't he stupid to advertise himself?" she sneered. "Even now the chain stinks of his pipe. What does he think I am? I may act stupid, all right, but I'll never be such a fool as to walk into this trap. He thinks there's not one foxy hair left on me. I'll pay him the same way I paid the badger for his house."

She assumed a picturesque pose, lifted her leg, and started to sprinkle the dead hare's head.

And then a mysterious voice whispered through the forest, the same voice that had spoiled her delight in mischief once before. A moist, gentle breeze, it did not churn the crowns of trees, did not shake branches, but slowly walked among the firs, larches, and pines, laying soft hands upon their heads, pressing them close as if in an embrace, and whispering intimate words: "Wake up! Come awake! Branches, revive! Buds, open your eyes! The joys of love are coming!"

And in answer, somewhere in the forest, a shy, small bird was heard; it chirped as if in a dream, and suddenly the entire forest echoed with sound, like a river when the ice breaks. The tops of two larch trees, vaulted by ice into a gothic arch, loosened their grip and swung apart. The gates of the unknown were opened.

Sharp-Ears froze. Never before had she felt a moment so sacred as this. What she was doing seemed a sacrilege. She crouched low to the ground, contrite and ashamed, expecting to be punished for her sin.

The vernal breeze strode past and disappeared toward the other slope. "Really," fumed Sharp-Ears, "I'm getting stupid." And she stamped her foot angrily.

Clack! answered the trap as it snapped shut on her bushy tail.

She called out the name of God, but it did her no good. The trap held fast, merciless, like iron. The hare's body had been flung aside, and the head now stared at her, its glassy eye asking, "Does it pinch?"

Horror rained cold upon Sharp-Ears, like dry, sandy snow. She couldn't stay caught here like this! She lunged up and shook the trap, but her tail was in agony. She could not even comprehend such pain. Only if she had suffered under a dentist's drill might she have known pain like this. In a frenzy, she jerked her body back and forth, and finally realized she would have to sacrifice the tip of her tail.

"No she-human would have the courage to do this," she said, trying to comfort herself. "She would sooner die than lose her beauty."

How can one describe the terrible operation that Sharp-Ears performed! It was not accomplished without sobs and tears, and when she finally seized her own splendid tail between her own teeth, as she had the humiliating rope that had tied her to the forester's doghouse, and bit through it, she wept bitterly.

"Never again will I get in man's way. Never again will I show myself in public. I'll huddle up to my nose in my den, and I'll stay there forever."

She could barely walk. Spots danced before her eyes, drops of blood like a shredded coral necklace spotted the snow behind her, as Sharp-Ears returned to her den, fighting tears. Before she lay down, she nursed her maimed tail and licked the wound clean.

"Will anybody want me without a tail?" She burst out weeping again, and all her heroism melted like snow. "But who would want me anyway? What am I talking about? Am I drunk? What is happening to me?"

By now, day was breaking. In their untidy nest in a twisted box tree an old sparrow couple was awake. Tenderly holding wings, they smoothed the ruffled feathers on each other's head with their beaks, like two people stroking one another's hair, and the old sparrow sputtered to his wife, "How many children have we had, old girl? Do you know?"

"How many children? Well, I don't know. I myself have had about thirty."

"And how many more will we have?"

"Oh, go to sleep. Somebody might hear you! You know animal tongues! The gossip will be all over the forest before morning!"

"Well, how many? Look here, you're still pretty . . ."

The old sparrow wife snuggled shyly up to her sparrow spouse, and with her wrinkled beak planted a loving kiss on his cheek. She whispered promisingly, "Wait. We'll talk about it in Maytime. That's when we'll have our silver wedding."

A lovely warm rain—not even a rain, only a gentle drizzle—filtered over the landscape. The snow was miraculously disappearing, singing torrents were gushing through every gully, patches of yellowish grass were peeking through the melting snowdrifts on the slopes, the lowland basin was filling with warm air like an enormous bridal bed being readied for the feast of love.

All the while Sharp-Ears was wiping the tears from her swollen eyes, sobbing until her body shivered.

"In Maytime . . ."

Forester Bartos could hardly wait until morning. He had slept badly, waking up often, and all night he had talked in his dreams.

"The devil knows what he's mumbling about all the time," grumbled his wife. "Maybe that Spanish thing's coming back."

When she heard him mumbling about Sharp-Ears, she was relieved, and she grabbed him by the shoulders and shook him awake. The forester started, waved his arms, sat up, and shouted in triumph, "I've got her! She's in heat!"

His wife put a cold compress on his head, and the forester fell asleep again, but he didn't stop jabbering. As soon as he woke up in the morning, he was in his trousers and dressed before you could count to ten, determined to get outside as fast as he could. Looking out the window to check the weather, he saw it was drizzling, and his face clouded to match the sky.

"Where are you off to in such a hurry? Where are the Furies sending you so early in the morning? You don't sleep, you toss and turn and fight with yourself all night, you don't rest like a human being!"

The forester fended off his wife and her worries. "Be quiet. I found her spoor. Today I'm going to bring Vixen Sharp-Ears home to you. Expect me back in an hour."

"For God's sake," exclaimed his wife, "don't bring her back alive!"

The forester took Catcher with him into the woods. He wanted to let his dog share the joy of victory over this adversary who had visited so many calamities upon them. On the way, though, his excitement began to ebb. Heavy mist fogged the valleys and ravines, the branches swayed in a nearly imperceptible breeze, and a sound resonated through the whole landscape—a hushed sound, like a baby gurgling in its cradle.

The pair reached the spot where they had set the trap yesterday and discovered the tip of Sharp-Ears's tail caught in it.

The forester kicked the hare so furiously that it flew into the trees. Then he shook his fist at the nosy Catcher and swore, not once but many times. The curses rolled from his mouth, thunder after thunder.

132

"I'm an old man," he wailed, "and that beast is going to mock me to death! From now on, I'll ignore her even if I trip over her!

But she'll come for her bullet, old rifle, I promise you that! Dog damn it, she's in heat. Someday I'll catch you off guard, Sharp-Ears, like I did your mother last year! And then we'll square our debt!"

Still cursing nonstop, he unchained the trap, picked it up, and stormed back to the village to seek consolation with the priest and the schoolmaster.

Heavy with catkins, the willows poured into the creek like a waterfall of liquid gold. All day they exhaled an intoxicating bittersweet perfume, and bees buzzed around from morning till dusk. The flowering branches, not wanting to fall asleep until late evening, stared into the moist, warm dark. The dark itself was in no hurry, and when finally it set out on its journey over forests, hills, and valleys, it seemed as reluctant to cover the earth as a gardener hating to lose one drop of sunshine and warmth, one who tries to seal up a hothouse of budding flowers but cannot. The darkness stepped into quiet glens, encountering shy deer as it went, spilled into the fields, and pressed its cheek against windowpanes, lighting the lamps inside and drawing families close together around dinner tables.

Following the dark, the moon swung high above tall pine trees, full and bright and looming large, shadows of elms and birch trees falling faint and blue in the clear lunar light. Songs resounded along the village roads—boys on their way to meet girls—and the moon paused as if bending its head in memory of bygone days when its rays had not yet cooled, when it, too, had hurried through the sky to meet someone, its blood excited and hot as the blazing sun.

The earth was falling asleep, though all things good and beautiful remained awake. Happiness and love never sleep, nor does silent sorrow which, like endlessly running rivers, turns the wheels of fortune and grinds the hard grain of destiny into soft bread.

A blackbird, like a living star, flies down to a barberry branch. He has survived the winter and now, when violets in the fields and blue windflowers on the hills are beginning to bud, he is feeling lonely. Enchanted and bewildered, he whistles his song composed of notes golden as the catkins of the willows and hazelnut bushes, touched with the purple of apple blossoms, pure as the white of endless rows of cherry trees, a song of warm nests and gently rustling branches. The song wells from his throat like droplets of blood—was there ever a human singer who could match him? And behold, a shy shadow flits among the branches: his future companion is approaching, filled with the desire to be joyful, to make him happy. He no longer sings for his own joy; he neither sees nor hears for the rapture of having been touched by spring. Only when he wakes the others, only when the rejuvenated earth bursts into life, only then will he stop, only then will he see her.

What is this change that comes over all of us in these moments? Unaware, we become brothers and sisters with the slim, young trees flowing with new sap, their gold-green leaves delicate and youthful as our dreams.

On such an evening, Sharp-Ears was wandering through the glen on her way to the creek. She had been ill ever since the day the forester's trap had caught her, and now she wanted to bathe her paws and her head. She had become reconciled to the loss of

135

the tip of her tail, her wound had healed, but she had been unable to shake the curious fever awakened in her by the vernal breeze. She could not know what was happening to her, for she had not experienced Maytime before and did not know how this fox illness was referred to by humans, who compose poetry only about themselves: humans sink under the burden of love; foxes just go into heat.

She had wandered like this many times before. Often she would lie on a rock warmed by the sun, press her body against it, place her snout on her paws, and whimper, her back bristling and her throat tight.

Today, after bathing in the creek, she felt as relieved as a maiden who has cried until her eyes are red. She surrendered herself into the arms of fate.

She was pleased to have lost weight, to have abandoned her former selfish gluttony, and was glad she was on her way to becoming a perfect creature, but if only she had someone to whom she could confide her sorrows! Lost in such thoughts, deaf and blind to her surroundings, she climbed a hillock near her den. She had not been here in nearly a week, and in the meantime the meadow had blossomed beautifully with lungworts, fumitories, and the first primroses. She paused and looked around with a melancholy glance and, at that moment, heard a slight rustle in the underbrush. But she did not run away. If forester Bartos himself had risen from the bushes, even if he had aimed his gun at her, Sharp-Ears would not have fled.

From the black dark of the thicket gleamed two glowing yellow eyes, and Sharp-Ears began to shiver all over.

"Dear God! He's so handsome!"

Sharp-Ears gasped and stared at him. "Him" was a muscular,

handsome male fox, such as she had never seen, not even in her dreams. His nobly shaped muzzle sported a dashing mustache, and a light-colored stripe ran between his ears. He walked with an elegant and youthful step, nonchalantly lashing his tail right and left as if twirling a fashionable walking stick. His fur was tough and thick, showing that he was no novice in this world, no young dandy just pushed out of mama's den.

Sharp-Ears felt a blush spread over her cheeks and muzzle, and was about to run away into the bushes when he addressed her in a rich, masculine baritone.

"Did I frighten you, miss?"

"Oh, nooooo," said Sharp-Ears.

"There certainly are a lot of bird's nests around here," he said, in an attempt to ease her embarrassment, and to demonstrate that he did not suspect her of some unbecoming springtime ramble.

"Uh-huh." She nodded modestly.

"Right now, though, there aren't too many here."

"Not too many. I know this spot very well. I live near here. I'm just taking a walk because I have a headache."

"Then allow me, please, to see you home. The hunters are all over the woods again, and when one is absorbed in thought and has a headache, one might easily come to harm."

"If you'll be so very kind," stammered Sharp-Ears in a whisper.

"That is, of course, if Madame Fox, your mother, won't be angry," he added hurriedly.

"Oh, nooooo," Sharp-Ears quickly replied. "I've been independent for a long time now. I even have my own house. My Uncle Badger bequeathed it to me."

The fox looked at Sharp-Ears with delight and genuine admiration, greatly surprised that such a young lady was independent and even had her own house. She obviously was naïve, inexperienced, unspoiled by the ways of the world and society, for in her touching innocence she kept shifting bashfully from one foot to another, not knowing what to do with her paws. His eye fell on the end of her tail, and in his heart he secretly rejoiced: she was courageous, too. And a good homemaker, well brought up.

Unable to conceal his admiration, he asked courteously, "Do you enjoy sports, miss?"

"Oh," she said with a charming smile, "and how! You'd be surprised how I can climb, but that's not proper in the presence of gentlemen. I used to climb into the pantry of the forester's house. I felt perfectly at home there."

"The forester's house!" He marveled and bowed respectfully.

"I grew up there. My upbringing is a bit human."

Astonished, he lowered his tail all the way to the ground. "Forgive me if I'm perhaps detaining you."

"Not at all," answered Sharp-Ears.

He bowed again, placed his left front paw on his chest, and, totally enchanted, introduced himself: "Golden-Stripe, the yellow-furred fox from the Deep Ravine."

"Delighted, sir! Sharp-Ears, the foster daughter of the forester's house."

She held out the tip of her right paw. Golden-Stripe kissed it ardently, stepped to her side, and together they headed toward her den. Golden-Stripe's heart was beating like a bell, and his head was spinning. He sensed that today he had met the greatest happiness of his life. They both were so excited that neither was able to say one sensible word throughout the entire journey.

Reaching Sharp-Ears's den, they stood helplessly, neither of them knowing what to do or how to begin. Golden-Stripe remembered that it would not be proper to bother a lady with conversation after a long walk, when she certainly wanted to rest, freshen up, perform certain necessities. So he started to leave. He could not, however, depart without saying something, and he could not go away without at least a spark of hope. Assuming a look of indifference, he brushed his virile mustache and asked politely, "Would you mind, miss, if I came to visit you again?"

"Of course not," answered Sharp-Ears, and blushed.

"Do you often go to the meadow?"

"Every day! It's my favorite walk after dinner, between midnight and one o'clock. Taking walks is my only pleasure. At the forester's house, they stopped liking me. I have no friends. I know no one in the neighborhood, so I walk by myself. Would you believe that I really walk all alone? I don't allow anyone to accompany me. I am proud of my independence."

"You are an absolutely ideal modern woman," said Golden-Stripe. "Do you, perhaps, also smoke?"

"Not yet."

"But perhaps you like to eat rabbits, miss?"

"Oh! And how!"

He knew all he wanted to know for today. For a brief moment he again felt embarrassed, not knowing how to take his leave, afraid of appearing either too cold and reserved or, worse, too intrusive and unsuitably forward.

"I kiss your hand," he finally said, considering this manner of farewell properly ceremonial. Prompted by respect, he ignored Sharp-Ears's readiness to part from him as if he already were a close friend; instead, when she offered her tail in a gesture of goodbye, he formally pressed the tip of it to his lips.

Sharp-Ears's preparations for bed that morning were unusually thorough. It was long past her bedtime, the sun was rising, and yet she was not sleepy. She rolled in sand to clean herself, combed every single hair, scratched out the burrs stuck in the fur under her neck—which required a lot of effort—smoothed the light hair of her summer coat, and only then slipped into bed. But she could not fall asleep. She lay on her back, smoothed out her tail, and stretched all four legs.

"Am I really pretty?" she asked herself. "What is nice about me?"

She was sorry that he had kissed the tip of her tail, where she had the ugly scar from the forester's trap. With shaking paws she gently touched her breast and turned over again. But her thoughts gave her no peace. She sat up, examined her whole figure with curiosity, and with a strict glance measured her hips. She smiled happily.

"I'm not that bad, after all."

She began to doze off contentedly when suddenly her eyes stared again. Some very strange fantasies had begun to plague her. Her head was full of wonderfully beautiful but at the same time horribly repulsive thoughts. God knows where they were coming from. Shame brought tears to her eyes. Why, she had caught herself puckering up her lips in sleep as if—fie!—as if she were trying to kiss someone!

She picked up some pebbles and began to pray fervently, as Mama Fox had taught her. She said as many Paternosters as there were pebbles.

Calmed at last, she dozed off into a chaste sleep.

140

Early in the evening, long before the moon rose, Sharp-Ears was up. As soon as she awoke, a maidenly blush reddened her cheeks, and with a delighted shiver she remembered last night's encounter. Swiftly she jumped out of bed and, humming a song, began to arrange herself carefully. She rubbed herself against a small, half-dry fir tree, splashed herself in a puddle, smoothed her head, made up her face a bit with dust from the road, and, when she was finished with everything, sat at her front window and looked out. She searched the sky anxiously for signs of rain, though it was still a long time until midnight. She never got up this early, and yet she felt vigorous and nimble as a squirrel. She thought of Anna back at the forester's house, who also used to prepare herself like this and impatiently curse everything that got in her way. As Sharp-Ears was daydreaming happily, the tender pine needles suddenly crackled and the branches rustled. Startled, she barely had time to recover when a familiar, pleasant male voice reached her ears.

141

"I kiss your hand!"

"Good morning. You got here early."

Golden-Stripe and Sharp-Ears stared at one another for a moment, as if comparing yesterday's memory with today's reality.

"She is so pretty, everybody in the ravine across the river will envy me. I mustn't let anyone steal her from me," he thought.

"You handsome hero, if you only knew what I dreamed and how much I have fallen in love with you," she thought.

Then they both laughed. It seemed silly, looking at one another like that for so long and saying nothing.

"Please," Sharp-Ears invited him, "do come inside."

Golden-Stripe hesitated. "Excuse me for not waiting until time for your walk," he said shyly.

"That's all right." She smiled. And casually, forgetting the refined manners she had assumed from the moment of last night's meeting, she added, "My feet hurt anyway."

Golden-Stripe leaped over the juniper bushes and said roguishly, "Here, miss, I've brought you something."

"You're terrible! Why are you taking so much trouble over me?"

"I caught it myself," he said, and with nonchalant chivalry laid a young rabbit at her feet. Then, debonairly curling his whiskers, he looked for the first time straight and lovingly at Sharp-Ears. His blood burned in his veins, so charming, so sweet she was, so simple and yet so pretty.

Sharp-Ears looked toward the rabbit, caught a swift glimpse of Golden-Stripe's splendidly masculine figure, and bashfully dropped her eyes. He, too, had carefully groomed himself, and his tail, strong as a young pine tree, was folded carefully around his hind legs and up to his chest.

Having overcome their initial shyness, the two sat down to eat,

142

chattering and bubbling with joy. The moon rose above the hillside. A blackbird flew up and hopped along a barberry branch above their heads, singing a song that pierced their souls. Sharp-Ears, wanting to prove herself an attentive hostess and to show her guest that she, too, knew how to hunt, brought a wild duck from her pantry, but could not find the words to ask her guest to eat. She shivered with happy excitement and a tear rolled down her muzzle. Golden-Stripe was no less moved, and so the duck remained untouched.

"Aren't you cold?" he asked, to cover his excitement, and his teeth chattered, not from cold but from desire. Silently he nestled closer to her.

"Noooo," whispered Sharp-Ears. "I'm very warm."

"Would you like to go for a walk tonight?" he asked in a trembling voice.

"I'm afraid," she breathed, and gazed timidly at him.

He bent his handsome head toward hers, folded his tail alongside hers, and, placing his first fleeting kiss on her ear, said to her passionately: "You, so independent, so bold, not frightened even of humans! You are afraid to go into the forest at night?"

Sharp-Ears was silent, but her heart beat violently.

"Shall we go?" he asked again.

"Uh-huh," she said distractedly.

And they went.

Not just one blackbird sang, but at least a dozen. A tree frog croaked in a puddle, ignoring the fact that, according to the almanac, she was not yet supposed to; a corncrake called; the starling, who had been out late drinking toasts to the arrival of spring, was still up, shouting at passersby and even hurling abuse at his own family; June bugs were holding a dance on wild apple

trees so covered with blossoms that the branches were invisible—
one never would believe that these working-class citizens, always
complaining of their poverty and low income, could carry on so.
The mosquito orchestra was tuning up. In a word, everyone was
celebrating international May Day with a general work stoppage.
Even the slovenly hedgehog could be seen rushing to join in, the
tip of a snail stuck to his whiskers. A secretive old drunkard who
bothered only about himself and left his wife to worry about the
family, he was disgracefully negligent about his person and had
not even taken the time to wipe his snout clean. The forest cross-
ings were jammed with animal pedestrians, and a screech owl
policing traffic kept shouting warnings in an attempt to prevent
collisions and accidents. Golden-Stripe and Sharp-Ears hurried to
get away from the commotion as fast as they possibly could.

They came out into a cool meadow on the edge of the forest,
where they found reassuring darkness. A cloud of mist was rising
from a drainage ditch bordered with thousands of buttercups.
Green frogs, with the kind cooperation of toads and tree frogs,
were engaged here in a sporting competition, and newts, chilly
and red from the cold, were offering the distinguished audience
flowers and refreshments.

Golden-Stripe, very attentive, presented Sharp-Ears with a
bouquet. She smiled at him gratefully. They talked about this and
that, and they marveled at how well they understood one another.
It was touching how their opinions on people, on hunting game
(both big and small), on catching mice and birds, coincided.
Only in their thoughts on love did the two differ.

"Have you ever loved?" asked Golden-Stripe cautiously.

"Noooo," she answered shyly. "Have you? A lot?"

145

"No! Never!"

"Why not?"

"Because I have not yet found someone whom I could respect, for whom I would give my life. But if I should find one like that, then . . ."

"And then?" asked Sharp-Ears with a catch in her throat.

"Then, without hesitating, I would say to her, Do you love me? Do you want me?"

Sharp-Ears was close to fainting. Her breath failed and she felt all four feet scrambling together. He embraced her just in time to keep her from falling.

"You are silent," said Golden-Stripe after some moments.

"Let go of me," begged Sharp-Ears, for his yellow eyes burned her and his paw around her waist felt like hot iron. "Let go of me, please let go of me, I'm afraid of you. You're horrible!"

"I'll let go if you wish, but I'm afraid you will fall."

"Take me back home!" she begged.

"Right away," he said, and now his heart was pounding, as hers had been earlier.

"Go away, I don't want to see you again. I'm afraid of you. You're terrible."

He let go of her, but he looked at her sadly and spoke: "Why don't you go—go and take away my happiness. You will ruin me, crush me. I don't want to live without you, not even one more day."

"Really? Why didn't you say that before?" she blurted out, and wiped her snout. She was melting with emotion, unable to move even a half step away from him.

146

"Yes, really. I've fallen in love with you, Sharp-Ears. It's you I love, you, my only one."

"Me, me," she whispered and sobbed. "Why me? Why me in particular?"

"Because you're just like the one I've always wanted. I'm not a liar, I'm not a sly, deceitful fox, Sharp-Ears, and I'm telling you what I've been carrying in my heart since yesterday. It's not your body, it's your soul I love. You are magnificent! Don't laugh, don't shake your head, you'll see, my Sharp-Ears! Novels will be written about us, and there will be people silly enough to read them to the end. Don't run away. Sit here beside me."

Sharp-Ears could not protest. She sat down, and Golden-Stripe grabbed her in his powerful embrace, pulled her gently onto his lap, and kissed her. Just as the raindrops fall, again and again his kisses fell.

"Don't cry. I, too, will cry for joy, my beautiful Sharp-Ears. Do you want me?"

She answered humbly, "I do."

147

It was not one or even two nights the happy lovers spent walking through woods and meadows—many nights there were, and sublime happiness walked with them. As soon as dusk began to fall and the first bat flashed over the treetops, Golden-Stripe arrived full of desire at Sharp-Ears's den. If she was still asleep, he sang to awaken her, and when she woke, he often covered her with kisses, although she resisted and fought him off because she wished to rinse out her mouth first. (Later on, he no longer would arrive to wake her, but would arise with Sharp-Ears.)

One day, she was behaving strangely. She refused to eat chickens, as if her gums were swollen. When Golden-Stripe, not wanting to bother her when she was feeling unwell, said goodbye, she came to him shyly and gently tugged the tip of his tail.

"What is it, my Sharp-Ears? You'll be lonesome if I leave, won't you?"

"And how!" she said wistfully.

"Then I'll stay a little longer."

Embarrassed, he sat on the threshold and watched two beetles wrestling under the stump. Suddenly Sharp-Ears ran off and he heard her hurriedly brushing her fur and changing her virginal bed.

"Ah," he said quietly. And he began to tidy himself, too.

Sharp-Ears sat on the bedside humming a song. He could not tell right away which one it was.

> *Dear boy, don't go out of sight,*
> *Stay with me throughout the night.*

Golden-Stripe stayed, not once or twice, but many times.

After that, their walks became shorter, but every stroll seemed more beautiful. Now they walked through ravines where they would meet no one. Sharp-Ears would nestle in his arms and he would softly embrace her, all the time whispering sweet words, joking about kisses, stars, her sparkling eyes; and she, lulled by his flatteries, would rest her head on his strong shoulder, kiss him furtively, and tease, "Wait, just wait! When you're a papa, what will you call Sharp-Ears then?"

"What will I call you? Mom. My old woman. That's what I'll call you!"

She slapped him over his ear because she didn't like coarse jokes, and she wanted him to love her in a pure way, to worship her, to approach her like a sacrament.

"You know that I was raised among humans," she often reminded him.

"You think that humans aren't just like us when they're in love? They're worse! They do everything for the sake of appear-

149

ances, to put on a show, but in reality they fight and quarrel like starlings when they've had their fill of love."

"But they write poetry, go to the theater and parties, get all dressed up . . ."

"And often, because they do, they don't even have anything to put in their mouths. People are nothing but pride, lies, and deceit. Not one single vixen can be as deceitful as a young girl tossing up her short skirts. No fox is as immoral as a handsome man-about-town. If one of us betrays his mate—but I won't do that, Sharp-Ears, you know I won't—then he runs away into another forest so the poor cast-off vixen doesn't even have to lay eyes on him. Man does just the opposite; he likes to keep running into his victim so he can degrade her, grind her into the mud, and then walk over her."

"And when something happens?" asked Sharp-Ears.

"They just pay off, and that's that. Our forest law won't permit that! Get lost or get married—pay with your self, not with your gold. And all the gossip that human mouths can produce! You, Sharp-Ears, would never be able to hold your own with humans if you loved one of them the way you love me!"

"But even so, I'm afraid of gossip right now. You know the owls, the gossipy jackdaws, and the sparrows."

"Just let them dare!" threatened Golden-Stripe.

No sooner were the words out of his mouth than an owl flew overhead, like an evil shadow.

"We're in trouble!" wailed Sharp-Ears. "See? Speak of the devil! I'm afraid of that bigoted hypocrite most of all. She knows how to tell her rosary, but she tells more tales than prayers."

150 Sharp-Ears's fears were justified. When the sun rose the next morning, the owl was sitting by her window, still not dressed, her gaudy woolen shawl over her shoulders, just the way she had

come rushing home from morning Mass, and on a branch in front of her sat a jay. They were telling enough tales and gossip to fill a bushel basket.

"You know, my dear," said the owl, "there is as much immorality today as there was in Sodom. It's almost as bad here in the forest as it is in the city. If you had seen what I saw, you'd have absolutely died of shame."

"What was it?" asked the jay, her eyes popping out of their sockets.

"Well, our little Miss Sharp-Ears—she always brags how she was raised by humans—is running around with a fox in the ravines, like the worst of them. Don't even ask me to tell you what I saw with these, my own eyes. Even at my age, I am ashamed to say it!"

"And with whom, pray tell me? She has always been such a nice vixen, she even was raised at the forester's."

"That's exactly it. It's bad enough that people don't want to know anything about God. They lock Him up in churches, poor thing, like a bird in a cage, when He would much rather be outside, under the open sky, among us, on every branch, on every blossom, in every flower cup. Those shameless, godless creatures cut Him out of wood like He was a breadboard, or they carve Him out of stone like He was a water trough. Fie! And they try to make you believe man was created in His image! Look at a human from above just once and you'll see for yourself. Is it possible, God forgive me for saying this, that He should be waddling around like a cripple, on only two legs, swinging his front ones like goose wings? Don't give me that kind of religion!"

"But what about Sharp-Ears?" the jay reminded her, burning with impatience.

"Oh, that. I forgot what I was talking about. Anyway, I saw them myself, my dear, and quite clearly. Mark my word, the two of them will come to no good end."

The owl leaned out of the window and, blinking her mean little eyes, told the jay every which and what, not leaving out a single scurrilous detail.

The jay listened in a trance. After she had heard it all, she flew straight off into the beech tree, where she knew she'd find the magpie, who was a prime gossip. The two whispered and hissed and didn't leave a single hair of Sharp-Ears's pelt untouched. They were so involved in scandal that they didn't notice the old starling on an adjacent limb, straining his ears to hear everything, his beak open as if he was lapping up every word, maliciously enjoying it all. Until now, he had been the major subject of neighborhood gossip, but—just wait!—now we see that the starling is not the only bad one! He is a saint, an angel compared to the other repulsive, base vermin. When he had heard all he wanted to hear, he made an evil face and sailed off to tell the sparrows without delay.

A whole flock of them were sitting down to breakfast as the starling flew into their midst with such speed that they scattered, alarmed, in all directions. Then they recognized him and began shouting at him, positive he was drunk again. The starling ignored their abuse.

"Hey, fellows!" he squawked viciously. "How'd you like to do a little dirt to somebody?"

"Sure! Sure! Sure!" chirped the sparrows, eager for any meanness.

"Then listen here, fellows! Our vixen is a slut!" he began promisingly, and was barely halfway into the story when the whole sparrow flock rose and flew straight to Sharp-Ears's den.

Don't ask how they carried on there! Such a ruckus of name calling hasn't been seen or heard in this neck of the woods for years—or anywhere else, for that matter. Before night came, the whole forest was gossiping. Even the sparrows sitting on the gutters of the forester's house were chirping about Sharp-Ears's sinful ways.

But humans, being so stupid, didn't understand a word.

153

Before Golden-Stripe set out to visit Sharp-Ears, he always prepared himself carefully, not only by shaking out and licking his fur, but also by a thorough planning of topics for discussion. He foolishly hoped to educate Sharp-Ears, just as callow students hope to improve their girlfriends, so that she would measure up more fully to his ideals; she, on the other hand, felt that her stay among humans had equipped her with a background that no other fox, anywhere, could match.

This evening, Golden-Stripe was in a poetic mood and had decided to discuss with Sharp-Ears the wondrous powers of music. But as he approached her den, he noticed that a change had taken place in the forest. Several squirrels sat in the old fir tree, and as soon as they saw him they all began poking one another and giggling. In the neighboring maple, the sparrows made faces at him, and the hedgehog, seated among the roots of the old stump, rudely stuck his tongue out at him. Golden-Stripe, unsettled, tried to concentrate on his plans.

Sharp-Ears was waiting for him. He kissed her warmly, stroked her forehead, and looked deeply into her eyes. They were red and swollen, and even the tip of her muzzle seemed drenched with tears.

"Sharp-Ears, my love, I have great news for you today," he began festively, but Sharp-Ears showed no curiosity. He added quickly, "Today I heard the first cuckoo!"

"Cuckoo!" she howled, and began to weep convulsively.

"Yes! A cuckoo! Does that mean something bad?" asked Golden-Stripe, astonished.

"How about a sparrow? You didn't hear the sparrows?"

"Why a sparrow?" he answered crossly. "Who ever listens to those rogues?"

Sharp-Ears sobbed aloud.

"What has happened, my love, my soul? Why are you crying?" he exclaimed in dismay.

"You don't know? You don't even suspect?" she asked bitterly, barely able to stand.

"No! For God's sake, don't torture me! Tell me!"

Poor Sharp-Ears bent her head toward his, tried to speak, fell into his arms, and resumed sobbing.

"Look at me and you'll see. It's your fault! I know why I was afraid of you! Remember? The first time we went for a walk together?"

Golden-Stripe looked, and his front paws dropped in astonishment. But because he was a noble soul, he recovered quickly and his eyes, too, filled with tears.

"What now?" she asked. "What are you going to do with me now?"

155

Golden-Stripe took a deep breath. "If it's like that, then the best thing to do is go straight to the priest."

Sharp-Ears did not object. Like a little child, she let him lead her where he wanted. They went through ravines, over hillsides, through meadows, until they finally arrived at a crossroads near a spring. There, all alone, stood an ancient mountain ash, his bark as white as a birch's. In his trunk gaped a black hole and next to it was a picture of the Virgin Mary, the Helping One. His bark was covered with initials left by tourists who had expressed their love-tortured, unhappy souls by carving long inscriptions. Here one could read, for example, "Frank has a crush on Josephine" or "Be it known to all in sight that I love you day and night." Down by the roots there was a low seat overgrown with grass. To this mountain ash in this lovely spot, a perfect site for nature's most exalted rendezvous, staggered the two lovers, one of the most unhappy couples this venerable tree had ever seen. Golden-Stripe cleared his throat and, plucking up all his courage, bravely knocked on the trunk.

"Who is it?" asked a deep and serious voice from within.

"Me and Sharp-Ears," answered Golden-Stripe.

The head of an old and distinguished woodpecker appeared. "Forever and ever, amen," it said, condescendingly acknowledging their humble Christian greeting. "It's time you finally thought of this. You took long enough."

Sharp-Ears again dissolved in tears.

"It's too late to cry now, my child," the forest priest reprimanded her, adding more gently, "It is, however, never too late for repentance. Just remember the beautiful penitent, St. Mary Magdalene. What is it you want?"

"Me? Maybe nothing," said Sharp-Ears mournfully. "Here. Ask him."

"We would like this . . . er, that . . . Reverend Father, we

156

would very much like a wedding," whispered Golden-Stripe almost inaudibly.

"You mean, rather, publishing the banns, don't you?" corrected the woodpecker.

"Well, then, the banns," agreed Golden-Stripe, slightly encouraged.

"You should have said it sooner. I guessed it when I saw you. All right, as you wish. We will do it nicely, as is fitting and proper for an honest family. Early in the morning, confession, the Holy Mass, and communion. After that, the wedding. Which day do you want to have it?"

"How about Saturday at noon? That's an elegant time," said Golden-Stripe. "Besides, we still have to invite our relatives—otherwise they'll think we're cheap."

"Right, right," agreed the woodpecker. "And now take your seat, Mr. Bridegroom, and you too, Miss Bride, and we'll take care of the catechism examination right away."

Golden-Stripe glanced furtively at Sharp-Ears and felt very sorry for her. Poor thing, she was standing there stiff as a stick, barely knowing where she was or what she was doing. He tenderly helped her take her seat and then sat next to her. The woodpecker straightened his biretta, then came out of the parsonage and called to his sexton, the nimble squirrel. The sexton knew how to climb the green vault of the forest cathedral, how to straighten the candles of the fir trees and the lamps of horse-chestnut blossoms, how to ring the tips of pine trees like bells, better than any human sexton ever could. Twilight was spreading through the forest, and the moment seemed holy enough to stop one's breath.

The priest was an old bird, rigid and severely ascetic, not a

157

politician like so many other priests who first serve their clubs and political party, and only after their meetings, card games, and other social events find the time to serve God. He had never had much to do with whining old women, or with young girls whom boys have cast off like half-nibbled cookies, leaving them to the bitter fate of becoming spinsters or else squandering their maidenhood as pilgrims and choir singers. The priest woodpecker hated that sort of thing from the bottom of his heart.

He took a pinch of snuff and blew his nose, lifted his finger threateningly, and asked the engaged couple one embarrassing question after the other, making them blush rather often. Sharp-Ears bitterly regretted her past offenses and sat there gloomily searching her conscience.

Golden-Stripe, who had sometimes toyed with atheism and freethinking, thought anxiously to himself, "Maybe there is something to this after all."

The woodpecker ended his examination and his lecture with an urgent command: "Now you will submit yourselves to fasting. Do not dare to sin again, as you have been doing. Remember that by receiving the sacrament, what was sin before now becomes a holy marital duty. You soon will have to care for a family; therefore, you must patiently tolerate one another's ways, loyally help each other, and not leave one another till death do you part. Do you promise?"

"We promise," breathed the happy couple.

"On Saturday, then, as you have decided, you will come to holy confession. Then in the company of the wedding party we will perform the ceremony which you so much desire. Now go in peace, and may God protect you."

The couple agreed that Sharp-Ears should move to Golden-Stripe's den in Hidden Valley after the wedding, for if they stayed in the neighborhood of the forester's house the little family would be in constant danger. The preparations for the wedding were carried out in a great hurry, just as humans do it. Golden-Stripe gathered relatives and invited guests, and like every bridegroom made a lot of mistakes, finally growing so confused that he complained to Sharp-Ears, who consoled him gently: "Look, husband, the forester used to say that I would go crazy. He was twice right—two of us went crazy."

The wedding itself was magnificent, so magnificent that we cannot even describe it—and besides, at least half the reading public, on their way through this vale of tears, has also experienced the pleasures and woes that go with a wedding. Anyway, everything that happened was reported all through the forest by the sparrows and explained by the owl, the magpie, the hedgehog,

159

the hares, the mice, and everyone else who came to gawk. Not even a forest wedding can escape gawkers.

The banquet was wonderful. A mixed choir of blackbirds, thrushes, finches, and robins even gave a vocal concert. There was no lack of toasts, and the bride and the groom survived them all in relatively good condition. Only one distantly related jackass of an uncle had disapproving thoughts and sent the blessed newlyweds a nasty letter.

One hot day while forester Bartos was tracking an animal, he came upon the vixen's deserted den. He was greatly pleased. He talked about it in Pasek's beer garden and in his heart he again promised his wife a muff made of Sharp-Ears's hide. To the schoolmaster he promised her dried tongue, which they say makes people invisible.

"It'll come in handy when you go courting sunflowers again," he pointed out.

"Not anymore," answered the schoolmaster sadly. "Miss Terynka is getting married today."

Surprised, the forester stared at his friend. But he could not see his face, for the schoolmaster had quickly turned toward the fence and, shielding his eyes with his hand, was looking fixedly away into the distance.

It was quiet today at Pasek's, nearly deserted. A dog was sleeping in the bowling alley, painters were working in the private room, father Pasek was in Brno, his wife seemed too busy to talk, and the priest, of course, was at Miss Terynka's wedding feast.

"We need the priest and his Latin," said the forester after a silent moment. Then he yawned, clinked his glass, paid, and rose to leave.

"Where are you going so soon?" asked the schoolteacher, his voice sounding soft and hurt, as if he had come to the end of a sad song.

"Where am I going? To the forest and then home. I didn't bring little Catcher with me today. His legs are hurting him, and he had to lie down. He's been like that ever since he got caught in the trap last winter. And he's getting old, my friend, just like we are. That's the way it is in this world. Last year we were full of fun and mischief, and this year we're glad to sit down somewhere and not budge."

He gently shook his friend's hand and soon was disappearing among the waving rye fields on his way to the Black Glen. He stopped by the last fence and shook his head. The schoolmaster, who was watching him intently, shook his head, too, his straggly hair flapping in all directions.

"Hope he didn't notice," he murmured, and blushed.

"Thunder and lightning," growled the forester at the same instant. "Dried up like a chip, and yet he can still squeeze out a tear. Never mind, old friend, you're better off. What would you do with a wife at this stage of life's game? That would be very bad counterpoint indeed."

Skeins of warm vapor hung lightly over the valley. There had been a small shower that morning, but now the warm sun shone happily again. On the moss and the brown pine needles, drops of dew were still glistening in rainbow colors, and the forester eagerly breathed in the heavy fragrance that wafted to him as he reached the edge of the stand of hornbeams.

"Mushrooms will be out," he thought, and leaving the path, he moved up the hill. "What did I tell you?" he said aloud after a while, and a squirrel scurrying somewhere through the treetops paused, full of curiosity. "Just like a painted toy soldier it stands.

And its chestnut top looks like the head of a young girl." The
forester joyfully stroked the healthy, slender mushroom.

With a light step he walked, with a light hand he picked the
mushrooms, while strange images and memories raced lightly
through his mind. Is it a fairy tale or is it true? How many years
has it been since two young people walked here, she as slim as

a fir tree, he as strong as a young oak? They had been gathering mushrooms, too, but they stepped on and crushed as many as they picked because they were blinded by love and could not see. But all the kisses they gathered!

"That was the day after our wedding," whispered the forester. "Dear God, the day after our wedding! When did you enlighten me, Lord? When was I wiser, then or now?"

He had reached the crest of the hill. There stood a curly growth of snowball bushes, privet, hawthorn, and dogwood, and in the middle of it all a mossy green hollow, soft as a plumped-up pillow embroidered with the words "Sweet Dreams."

The forester stared at the hollow and sat down, leaned his rifle against his knee, and lost himself in thought.

"If it weren't for the flies, a man could fall asleep in a second," he mused, still in his pensive mood, and stretched himself out. "It's a good thing they won't let me sleep. I'd get home late again." And in a minute he was fast asleep.

What a vivid dream he had! He saw the golden-green foliage of the forest open, the curtain of branches part. A narrow, sunlit clearing appeared, and in it an ancient mountain ash with a holy picture on the trunk, an old woodpecker waving his claw from a hole in it. Below, foxes lined up neatly in pairs; above them, a cloud of tiny singing birds; around them, groups of animals large and small.

"A wedding!" breathed the dreaming forester. "Glory be, they're carrying on just like people! Look at them! Those stags are even wearing horns!"

Then he saw the banquet and noticed that animal tongues, too, are loosened, and snares of love tightened, just as among humans.

163

"Leave her alone!" he heard himself shout to a sly fox who, unnoticed by the feasting relatives, was trying to lure a nimble, fiery young vixen into a nearby ravine. The colorful images went on and on, and the forester couldn't take his eyes off the scene, all the while searching for her . . . for Sharp-Ears.

"Hey! There she is!" he shouted.

She was not alone. A flock of cubs surrounded her. There was Little-Tail, Feather-Catch, and little Golden-Stripe, who was the spitting image of his father, and even a grinning, spoiled, baby Sharp-Ears looking like the one he caught last year.

"Just wait! I'll get you!" he decided. "Like I got your mama! But I'll raise you better, so they won't write about you and me in newspapers and novels again!"

He sat up and threw out his arms, but his hands clasped nothing. He realized he was no longer dreaming, that he was awake, that it was getting dark, and that he was sitting in a lovely, mossy hollow. A frightened young green frog darted in front of his nose.

"Eh, you cold monster! Where did you come from, dog damn it?" exploded the forester.

"Tha-tha-tha-that wasn't m-m-m-me! Tha-tha-tha-that was my grandfather! He used to tell me ab-ab-ab-about you!" stammered the terrified frog. And rolling its eyes in fear, it dove into the underbrush.

And so our simple story ends. But there is no way of discovering for certain how it all really ended. Our dear readers, however, can find out for themselves. We say "dear readers" because the dear writers of olden days used this gallant, charming term even when their readers may not have been dear at all. But it was a nice custom, and it will hurt no one to bring it back now for our farewell. And so, dear readers, when you air your furs to rid them of destructive moths, please examine the ends of their tails. Should a tip be missing, or if one was added on, perhaps you hold in your own hands the remains of that cunning little vixen, Sharp-Ears.

AFTERWORD

Vixen Sharp-Ears was a real fox who had real adventures with a real forester sometime in the nineteenth century. She was known and loved by the Czech country folk long before an artist named Stanislav Lolek and an unhappy newspaperman named Rudolf Tesnohlidek immortalized her in a newspaper serial that inspired Leos Janacek to write one of the greatest twentieth-century operas about her: *The Adventures of Vixen Sharp-Ears*, better known in English-speaking countries as *The Cunning Little Vixen*.

Tesnohlidek's novel is no fairy tale. It presents a world of not-so-innocent animals living out their short lives in brutal harmony alongside a world of longer-lived humans who are no less brutal, scarcely more intelligent, and a good deal less happy. Neither Tesnohlidek's animal nor human world is an ideal one, but it is his genius that he is able to lead his readers to an acceptance and final understanding of nature's grand design, just as he has led his hero, the forester Bartos.

The theme of *The Cunning Little Vixen* is eternal life: not life-after-death in the religious or reincarnationist sense, but endless rebirth according to nature's self-renewal. It is a pantheistic attitude, this identification of God with all that is contained in the universe, and it is typical of many literary works written by authors who have been close to the earth. Country people, scratching out an existence from the land, living in the midst of forests and mountains and rushing streams, were—and still are—able to sense the presence of God in the world of nature in a very real way. The haunted, unhappy Tesnohlidek sought relief from his considerable woes in nature; the church-hating Janacek filled his works with references to God while loudly denying His existence and worshipping nature as only a true pantheist worships it. It is no wonder that these two pantheists, both Moravians and living in the same city, embraced Sharp-Ears and her animal world, seeing in it a purity and truth that they knew are missing from the more sophisticated society of humans.

Rudolf Tesnohlidek was born in Caslav, a small city about fifty miles east of Prague, on June 7, 1882. His first experiences with animals were hardly pleasant: his father was a knacker and earned his living by dispatching ailing and unwanted animals, then skinning them and tanning their hides. Young Rudolf often ran from the screams of dying beasts and hid in the garden outside his house. That may have been the reason he felt less close to his father than to his mother, whose own father was a veterinarian. The elder Tesnohlidek's unappealing profession had the effect of placing the entire family at the bottom level of local society. Said Rudolf in later years: "My father's occupation cast an evil shadow over my life. It made me shy, and I still do not feel at ease in society. I look at it through the eyes of an outcast."

As if that weren't handicap enough, Rudolf suffered from an eye problem that gave him a strange, almost manic appearance: his eyes would spin around, darting uncontrollably this way and that. He grew up introverted and oversensitive, a voracious reader inclined to find refuge in books, especially books of poetry.

In the summer of 1901, the first storm clouds began to gather. Tesnohlidek went swimming one day with his friend Filo Weber, and suddenly, while standing on the shore watching his companion in the water, he realized that Filo was in serious trouble. Filo was, in fact, drowning, calling desperately to Rudolf for help. As the enormity of the situation swept over Tesnohlidek, his muscles locked and he stared immobile at his friend floundering in the water. Finally, Filo sank out of sight, leaving the nineteen-year-old Tesnohlidek to spend the rest of his life in guilty self-accusation.

About the same time, his mother died, and the elder Tesnohlidek re-

168

married. No love was lost between Rudolf and his stepmother, and there was general relief when Rudolf announced he would not enter the priesthood as he had been planning, but would try his luck in the city. He headed for Prague with an inheritance from his mother, enough to keep him for three months, and began earning money as a tutor. Meanwhile, he studied philosophy and languages at the university and soon experienced the once-in-a-lifetime thrill of seeing his first work in print. This was a collection of resoundingly gloomy verses published under the pseudonym Arnost Bellis.

There was nothing unusual about Tesnohlidek's literary gloom, for it was very much the style of the time. Turn-of-the-century Prague was drenched in melancholy, with such non-Czech figures as Edgar Allan Poe and the Symbolists Baudelaire and Maeterlinck setting the pace in literature. Morbidity was the fashion, pessimism virtually a religion. Tesnohlidek's stylish sadness gloried in such lines as "Somewhere in the dusk, the evening falls in heavy darkness filled with sorrow."

The sorrow was lightened somewhat by the attractive person of Jindra Kopecka, whom Tesnohlidek met in 1902. Kaja—the nickname came from her initials—was beautiful, strong-willed, and literary. She had inherited money from her father and illness from her mother. Formerly bright-natured, she had taken on the fevered intensity of a Lady of the Camellias, and her enthusiasm for literature and the other arts had turned her into a creature as stylishly somber as even Tesnohlidek could wish. Suicide being a currently admired exit from this world, Kaja expressed her hopes in these Wertheresque terms: "I should like to leap into the river, under the ice, and drift with the floating ice floes toward the distant sea. That way, nobody could ever find me and I could stay there alone forever."

The two young people fell in love, and on May 23, 1905, were married. A woman of force, Kaja was thought by most of their friends to have been

169

responsible for leading Tesnohlidek to the altar, an opinion reinforced by her comment as they rode off after the wedding. "According to the Bible," said Kaja on their way across Prague's Charles Bridge, "the wife should follow the man, but in this case it's the other way around."

But the two young people obviously seemed destined for each other. Kaja, twenty-five, and Rudolf, twenty-three, had similar tastes and even made plans for a joint career translating the Scandinavian authors they loved. Their favorite was Alexander Lange Kielland, who lived and wrote in the Norwegian village of Molde, and it became both a pilgrimage and a honeymoon when Rudolf and Kaja decided to go to Norway in July, just two months after their wedding.

It was a major journey in those days, and the couple's excitement can easily be imagined. The only dark cloud came when they told Kaja's grandmother about the trip. The old lady dabbled in spiritualism; she consulted the "other side" and informed the surprised couple that, according to the spirits, Kaja not only was going to a northern country but would remain there. Despite this odd prophecy, the Tesnohlideks went ahead with their plans, celebrating their last night in Prague with a climb up the hill to Hradcany (Prague Castle) to have a romantic look at the city by moonlight. On their way home, they heard a distant piano playing a funeral march by Grieg and, since Grieg was Norway's most famous composer, took it to be a happy omen. Rudolf even sang the words to Kaja. "I found in her more than I ever hoped for," he wrote. "Her *tristesse* had a special, irresistible charm for me."

The Tesnohlideks left Prague on July 8. Once in Norway, they learned of the picturesque town of Vestnes and decided to visit it as a side excursion. A fellow vacationer in the hotel in Molde, a young doctor named Nils Parelius, saw them off and described what happened next:

170

About ten o'clock in the evening, while it was still daylight, a man arrived from Vestnes. He was out of breath and asking for my father. I

asked him why. "A foreign man in the Vestnes hotel shot his wife."
I knew immediately that this man could be no one but Tesnohlidek. I
did not believe that he was capable of doing this, but of course that
meant nothing. I learned from the man that he had been arrested, im-
prisoned, and was now waiting for the Commissioner. My father, a
courtroom physician, was home—he ran off and in a little while was in
a motorboat rushing to Vestnes. He returned in the morning with
Tesnohlidek, who was more dead than alive, tearful and in despair, and
really to be pitied. My father told us how the tragedy had occurred.

The young people had settled in a room with a veranda, which Mrs.
Tesnohlidek liked. They ate supper, and the lady went through the door
that led from the room to the veranda, so she could see where they were
going to go walking. At the same time she was playing with her revolver,
a small one like a child's toy, which she had on a chain. Tesnohlidek
watched her from the room and asked her to lay down the weapon
because something could easily happen.

The lady just smiled. "What could happen?" she supposedly asked.
"You might shoot yourself," he answered, worried. "And do you think I
wouldn't have the nerve to do that?" his lady asked. "I have the nerve."
She released the safety catch and pointed the weapon at herself, her
finger on the trigger. Here Tesnohlidek raised himself with the words
"Don't joke like that, don't torture me!" and leaped toward her. At that
moment a shot exploded, and she sank to the ground, dead. She was shot
right in the heart.

An autopsy revealed that Kaja would have died soon anyway, for her
lungs were virtually destroyed by tuberculosis. She was buried in Vestnes,
and Tesnohlidek was brought to trial there, dismaying everyone with his
rambling, contradictory testimony. Like a shellshocked soldier, Tesnohlidek
confessed only to being thoroughly bewildered by his wife's death. He kept
repeating that he had not always been successful in understanding her,

adding the curious information that suicide was quite common among Czechs, who, he said, were always doing it for rather minor reasons. Later, he went through still another trial. Again his testimony was a florid shambles, and again he was acquitted. When it was all over and he returned to Prague, he refused to go back to his and Kaja's old apartment, abandoning whatever keepsakes were there and giving up all rights to his wife's estate rather than face the legal complications. As for Kaja's family and friends, he couldn't face them either, and so avoided them.

From then on, Tesnohlidek was a changed man. "He was always sad, uneasy, spoke to no one," recalled Alfred Tesnohlidek, his brother. "His Jindra shone like a star in the labyrinth of life—she shone and then was extinguished. Wretchedness and darkness overtook Rudolf. Because of our father's profession, we were looked down upon by everyone, like outcasts of society, and it hurt to be among people. Whenever Ruda and I met again, he was always closed unto himself and did not permit a look into his innermost being—his future life was only a puzzle to me."

In 1908, Tesnohlidek met Arnost Heinrich, chief editor of *Lidove Noviny (People's News)*, an important newspaper in Brno, largest city of Moravia and second largest city of what is now Czechoslovakia (current population: 369,000). Heinrich offered Tesnohlidek a job as court reporter, and the depressed, nearly starving man snatched at it.

Tesnohlidek's prose took on a gloomier aspect, and his books, poems, and plays began to reek with melancholy. He also began to write in the distinctive Brno dialect, which is virtually unintelligible to non-Brnians. At one point he showed some of his poems to Jaromir John, an editor of *Lidove Noviny*, and John was shocked at the depths of their pessimism: "It was a finely filed key to his soul, an urn filled to the brim with sorrows that had not yet been cremated."

In 1910, Tesnohlidek married a young woman of eighteen, then fathered a son and adopted a daughter, but the marriage failed after a few years.

Anna Tesnohlidek was bright and extroverted and liked parties and the theater, while Rudolf preferred solitary strolls through the forest. Anna eventually ran off with a doctor Tesnohlidek had met while covering the Balkan Wars for his newspaper.

He had better luck with Olga Zamecnikova, his third wife. He had been friends with both her and her husband before the two were divorced, and he waited a discreet year before marrying her. A schoolteacher, she was of a new generation, and he began to rebuild his life around her, helped along by the popular success of *The Cunning Little Vixen*, which was serialized in *Lidove Noviny* in 1920. But he was beginning to show signs of mental instability. Matters worsened when Heinrich, his editor, rewarded the *Vixen* triumph by informing Tesnohlidek that he was being relieved of his usual courtroom reporting, that a younger man was taking over the assignment, and that he should be pleased to have more free time.

Tesnohlidek was appalled. What he needed was not free time but assurance that he was indispensable. He began a pathetic campaign to coax kindness out of Heinrich, who was not fond of coddling neurotic writers: twice a year, Tesnohlidek would resign, and Heinrich would angrily refuse to accept his resignation. When Tesnohlidek would ineptly hint that he had a better offer, Heinrich would gleefully congratulate him and bid him goodbye. Co-workers always saved the situation, smoothing over relations between writer and editor, but by then Tesnohlidek had become a haunted, bitter man, and rather a trial to his colleagues.

Jaromir John was more patient. He would listen to Tesnohlidek's complaints and ask, "Do you have anything better in Prague?"

"I don't."

"Are you looking for other jobs?"

No answer.

"So what are you going to do?"

"I don't know."

"He manufactured sadness on purpose," recalled Jaromir John. "Rudolf came from a generation which loved to cultivate sadness, even unto self-destruction. He was physically and emotionally created for literary self-flagellation. In the newspaper office we considered him odd, an eternal pessimist. The fate of such people is difficult. Soon they begin to bore even the kindest person who feels for them."

His co-workers began avoiding Tesnohlidek—the deadline frenzy of a busy newspaper office is hardly conducive to deep friendships in any case. Tesnohlidek developed an interest in hypnotism and became convinced he was hallucinating. A trapped look settled on the face of Olga Tesnohlidek and it was obvious that matters were fast deteriorating.

Suddenly Tesnohlidek found something to be enthusiastic about. "He took himself to the caverns in Slovakia, which were just being discovered," wrote John. "*Lidove Noviny* was swamped with articles about the monumental caverns that he explored. It was useless to talk to him. He withdrew into himself, obsessed with caverns. 'Caverns again!' complained the men over his lengthy copy. They cut his stories to a minimum and sometimes threw them into the wastebasket, never suspecting that he was burying himself alive in the deadness of the earth, that he was searching for the womb in the ground, that for four years he crawled through the cold, wet interior where the stalactites, minute after minute, shed tears. With his words Rudolf searched for an abyss which would swallow him in silence, blessed forgetfulness, and quiet eternity."

Tesnohlidek found final forgetfulness on January 12, 1928. Among his jobs was the writing of a set of humorous verses for each Saturday edition. On that last Thursday, before the noon deadline for the Saturday paper, he wrote a farewell to the world, phrased it in his funniest manner, shaped it to the length of his weekly column, and put it on his desk. By the time he had finished, most of the staff had gone to lunch. Tesnohlidek added an apologetic note: "Don't be angry that I did it here. I didn't want to spoil her little nest, because I still love her very much, until my last moment, and here I spent twenty years."

Then he shot himself in the chest. Bleeding profusely, he got up and walked down a long corridor, found a clerk, and asked for a doctor. He died shortly afterward. When the news was broken to Olga Tesnohlidek, she locked the doors, turned on the gas, and followed her husband into oblivion.

Was Rudolf Tesnohlidek a murderer? Many people thought he was, and that a guilty conscience lay at the root of his mental problems. But in Tesnohlidek's time, suicide was viewed as a terrible thing, with heavy blame heaped on the head of anyone who might have prevented it. It seems likely that Kaja Tesnohlidek actually shot herself, either in play or in depression, and that her distraught husband tried so hard, and so clumsily, to explain her death that he ended by casting suspicion upon himself. But the general opinion was expressed by Jaromir John after Tesnohlidek's death: "He was pursued by the worst of all the vengeful Furies—Tisiphone, avenger of murder—and he finally, to appease her, entered her abysmal abode and never returned."

Tesnohlidek wrote a number of books, poems, and plays, many of them still read in Czechoslovakia. His translations of Scandinavian authors are held in high esteem; his children's books (*The Cricket's Travels* and the melancholy *New Kingdom*) are still read with pleasure; and his strong, realistic *Kolonia Kutesjik* is regarded as a minor classic of Czech literature (it won the Czechoslovak State Prize in 1922).

None, though, fired the popular imagination as did *The Cunning Little Vixen*, a joyful tribute to the forces of nature, colored only slightly by melancholy. (Given his tragic life story, it comes as a surprise to learn that Tesnohlidek was considered a first-rate humorist for a publication whose motto was "The Newspaper for Happy Reading.") The true story of Sharp-Ears, at least in its essentials, had come to Tesnohlidek through the work of the Czech landscape painter Stanislav Lolek, who had met a game warden, or forester, named Korinek, in the mid-1880s. It was Korinek who told Lolek about the trio of card-playing friends who spent convivial evenings in the tavern U Jelena (The Stag), the forester and his grandson, their dog, and their encounters with an unruly vixen. The story struck nostalgic chords in Lolek's memory, for he had served as a forester's assistant in Bohemia before he went to Prague to study art. Lolek liked the tale so much that he dashed off nearly two hundred sketches of it, in later years adding an oil painting called *The Fox Family*. In the 1880s, however, Lolek was still a student, and though he saved his sketches of the fox story, he never liked them very much and kept them hidden from sight.

In late 1919, while Tesnohlidek was writing for *Lidove Noviny*, the newspaper announced that it would become the first Brno newspaper to carry pictures. "In every morning and afternoon edition there would be a picture with some funny text," wrote Jaromir John. "That would make twelve pictures a week, which, with one or two stories, would be enough to fill a whole weekly. It was a difficult assignment for those days. I procured all the painters in Moravia, and on one excursion I traveled to Prague and Stanislav Lolek."

Lolek claimed he had nothing suitable. In fact, he seems to have been thoroughly uninterested in *Lidove Noviny*'s project and insisted that he was a painter of landscapes and could not draw figures. On the verge of leaving empty-handed, John noticed a pile of paintings, sketches, and magazines, the whole heap crowned by an ancient and dusty sweater. John pawed through the mess and at floor level found a fat package of sketches:

176

I brushed it off and looked. There was a series of drawings of a furious game warden with angry whiskers and some kind of a hunted vixen.

I stuffed it under my arm and, paying no attention to the protesting Lolek, sped to the railroad station.

I was very happy when I examined the drawings in the station restaurant. Not a page was missing. The story was complete and well suited for newspaper reproduction. "I'll add a text and stretch this adventure for at least a quarter of a year!" I got to Brno at almost four in the morning and went directly to the office. Heinrich was sitting there with some friends and a bottle of wine.

Heinrich hit the ceiling when he saw the drawings. For some reason he hated them on sight, called everyone incompetents, and demanded to know what they all expected him to do with such stuff. Informed that the pictures already had been paid for, he shouted, banged his desk, and terrified everyone. The offending pictures thereupon vanished, to surface every few days for several weeks, until finally Heinrich, with deadly sweetness, dropped them on Tesnohlidek's desk and said, "We must have some text for this."

Tesnohlidek stuffed the pictures into his briefcase. "This was a book I was mad at," he later recalled. "Nobody wanted to write it, but one day in February 1920 I finally started." His first draft of the opening chapter was not good, and he threw it away. "I went out into the woods, and it was a beautiful warm day, almost like spring. I listened to the dialect the woodcutters were talking, then I began to write again."

And Sharp-Ears worked her magic afresh. "Soon I was scribbling so furiously that the printers couldn't keep up and threatened to go on strike," said Tesnohlidek. "Finally I was ordered to dictate it. That's when I realized how useful it is to hear one's own sentences."

Tesnohlidek placed the action of his story in the forests north of Brno, in the Moravsky Kras, where he often walked alone. The villages in the story—Vranov, Ricmanice, Krtiny—are actual villages, and the forester's lodge is popularly supposed to be the one named Jezirko (Little Lake) that still stands on the road from Sobesice to Utechov. As he wrote, Tesnohlidek moved beyond the simple cartoon style of Lolek into a soaring pantheism that verged on poetry. Like all great comedies, his story is tinged with tears and warmed by compassion for his characters. Furthermore, he filled it with satirical allusions and double meanings, many involving the social and political upheavals of Czechoslovakia immediately after the First World War. To better appreciate his jibes, one should know that Moravia, Bohemia, and Slovakia had been part of the Austro-Hungarian Empire and under the domination of the Hapsburg dynasty for centuries. German rule was very harsh (in some regions the Czech language was even outlawed, in an attempt to wipe out Czech culture), but in 1918 the end of the war brought the unification of Moravia, Bohemia, and Slovakia: the Republic of Czechoslovakia was born. Byproducts of the Republic were the legalization of divorce and the growing importance of the Communist Party.

The only passages that might puzzle non-Czech readers are those involving the birth of the mosquito and his later exchange with the green frog: black and yellow were the colors of the hated Hapsburgs; green was the color of the powerful new Agrarian Party. The Eagles and the Children of Mary were organizations of Catholic youth that were not looked upon kindly by the anti-clerical Tesnohlidek; hence, the sardonic comment that the two organizations made a tavern their "nest."

By the time Tesnohlidek finished his little novel, it boasted something for nearly everybody: charm, suspense, fun, double meanings, barbs hurled at church and state, and a heroine who was emphatically irresistible. Tesnohlidek named both his heroine and his book *Liska Bystronozka (Vixen Fleet-Foot)*, but at the last moment a typesetter misread the word, and *Bystronozka* came out *Bystrouska*—"Sharp-Ears." Tesnohlidek thought the new name just as good as the old and let it stand. (The more evocative *Cunning Little Vixen* is from the German title [*Das Schlaue Füchslein*] of Janacek's opera, a name supplied by Max Brod, creator of the German version for Janacek's Viennese publishers.) As *Vixen Sharp-Ears*, the story bounded into print for the first time on Wednesday, April 7, 1920, appearing roughly twice a week until it ended on Wednesday, June 23, 1920. "When publication began," said Tesnohlidek, "I couldn't believe what was happening. People just went crazy over Sharp-Ears. I began getting hysterical letters, postcards full of rude words, others full of praise." By popular demand, the story was published in book form a year later, with Lolek's illustrations and some minor revisions—a word here, a phrase there—by Tesnohlidek. It has been in print ever since, often in competing editions.

The story was a natural for Leos Janacek, who had been born in Hukvaldy, a minuscule village near the Polish border, where he still had a vacation house, but who had lived in Brno since he was eleven. Janacek's rotund little body and shock of bristling white hair (he was sixty-eight in 1920) had long been a familiar Brno sight, and his reputation as a choral director, a Czech nationalist, a collector of folk songs and speech patterns of both people and animals, and a composer of operas that seemed hopelessly strange to most people had assumed an aura of near-legend. In 1916, he had become internationally famous with his opera *Jenufa*, written sixteen years earlier.

As a personality, Janacek was the polar opposite of Tesnohlidek. Janacek was excitable and optimistic, given to storms of rage and torrents of enthusiasm. He was generally adored despite a scandalous private life (he relieved an unhappy marriage with numerous affairs) and his shocking attitude toward religion. He loathed organized religion and preferred his own passionate kind of nature worship. Janacek loved dogs and chickens and even managed to train his hens, dim-witted creatures if ever such existed, to scratch in the proper places. He was once observed pursuing a flock of birds by dawn's earliest light, scribbling down their calls in a note-book and pleading with them, "Speak to me, please speak to me! I must have your music! I must have it!"

It is hard to believe that such a man was one of the last people in Brno to read about Sharp-Ears. Yet, if Marie Stejskalova, his housekeeper, is to be believed, it was her idea to make an opera out of the vixen's story. As Stejskalova reports in her memoirs:

The morning edition of *Lidove Noviny* was delivered to our home, the afternoon one I used to fetch from the tobacco shop. At the time of *Sharp-Ears*, I used to open the paper on my way home to see if there was a new part in it, and when there was one, I ran home, read it quickly, and only then gave the paper to the master. He was working anyway and would only get to the newspaper in the evening. Once I was reading it and there was this picture of Sharp-Ears and Golden-Stripe, arm in arm, and she was carrying a bouquet of flowers. I found it very funny, the way they were posed. I thought that nobody could hear me and laughed aloud. The mistress was not at home, and the master was in his study. But suddenly he was standing at the kitchen door.

"Tell me, please, what are you laughing so hard at?"

"At Sharp-Ears, sir."

"What Sharp-Ears?"

"Oh, aren't you reading it? It is by Mr. Tesnohlidek, from *Lidove Noviny.*"

I handed him the paper. He looked at the picture, read the text, began to smile, and I said: "Sir, you know so well what animals say, you always copy down bird voices, this would make a wonderful opera!"

He said nothing. But from then on he was always looking for the next installment of *Sharp-Ears*. And what didn't happen! He went to see Mr. Tesnohlidek, and then the latter came to our house, they reached an agreement, and our master began to study the animals for *Sharp-Ears*. He would get up at six in the morning, drink his mineral water, and go to Luzanky Park to listen to the singing of birds, to the humming of trees, to the buzzing of bumblebees. He used to come back enlivened and cheerful: "What people miss when they sleep!"

If Tesnohlidek was surprised at the sudden fame of his work, he was downright flabbergasted when Janacek wanted to make it into an opera. As he wrote:

Vixen Sharp-Ears has played her tricks even in the newspapers, and I do not know why people like her so much; perhaps because she keeps well to the ground. It would never have occurred to me that she had a diligent reader and admirer, a man with silver hair and sparkling eyes. I knew him only distantly, because he is a musician, and I do not pretend to understand music. Suddenly I heard that the vixen had bewitched him and that he wanted her trivial words and even more trivial actions transcribed into the language of notes, which is, of all human things, the least earth-bound.

I could not believe it and took it for a joke. Later I was assailed by a direct demand: What would I have to say to it? I said nothing. I was surprised and had the feeling that someone was trying to play a trick on me. Then one spring day I received an invitation from Janacek himself.

My heart was heavier than the heart of Sharp-Ears when she got caught in the pantry. I gathered all my courage and went. It was a May day and the song of the birds filled the air over the streets and roofs of Brno just as if it were somewhere in the meadows down by the Svitava River.

Leos Janacek was waiting for me in the small garden of the Conservatory. He sat among the bushes, with thousands of tiny blossoms blazing around his head; that head of his was equally white and seemed the biggest of those flowers. He smiled. And I immediately knew that this is the smile which life presents to us like a gold medal for bravery in the face of the enemy, for bravery in sorrow, adversity, and anger. At that moment I believed that Vixen Sharp-Ears was sitting tamed and quite dominated by the kindness of the man in the small garden, and that she would approach unseen to sit at our feet and listen to our plotting.

The nature-loving Janacek enthusiastically threw himself into Tesnohlidek's animal world. He often went to his cottage in Hukvaldy, where his friend, the forester Vincenc Sladek, obligingly located a family of foxes for him to spy on. He finished writing his libretto in the autumn of 1922 and completed the music on April 3, 1923. Said Janacek: "I wrote *The Adventures of Vixen Sharp-Ears* for the forest and the sadness of old age."

Janacek's opera follows Tesnohlidek's story very closely, though it omits (for reasons of brevity as well as obvious stage practicality) the vixen's raids on the chicken coop, the forester's hilarious manure bath, the ensuing pig feast, and the uproarious battle in the pantry (the vixen describes the latter, however, when she tells Golden-Stripe the story of her life).

The opera's first act comprises the vixen's capture, her adventures with Catcher and the chickens, and her escape. The second act opens with the ousting of the badger, continues with the humans' drinking bout, and finishes with the meeting of Sharp-Ears and Golden-Stripe and their wedding, a ceremony that brings down the curtain on a scene of merriment.

Janacek's last act departs from Tesnohlidek in several ways. He fuses the poacher Martinek and the merchant Harasta into a single character, then has the forester lay his trap, but without injuring Sharp-Ears. He then brings on the vixen and her husband and cubs. A tender family scene follows, with the fox pair speaking the lines that, in the novel, are delivered by the old sparrow couple, and then Janacek draws the opera to a shocking climax: Harasta shoots Sharp-Ears, and she falls dead at the peak of her happiness. Her death, though, is not so drastic a change as it seems at first glance. Tesnohlidek's final paragraph hints that something of the sort may have happened, and Janacek merely fulfills the original hint of doom by turning his heroine into a muff that is given to Terynka as a wedding present. More important, the vixen's death is a dramatic masterstroke on Janacek's part, and it endows the final pages of the opera with almost unbearable poignancy.

After Sharp-Ears's death, the opera proceeds as does the book, with the melancholy scene in Pasek's tavern, then the forester's walk into the woods. Here Janacek caps his opera with a meditative soliloquy for the forester, taking his text from Tesnohlidek's more poetic passages. The heart of the soliloquy is the forester's vision of Maytime—Tesnohlidek's paragraph beginning "How splendid stood the forest!"—which Janacek builds to an ecstatic musical climax. The green frog's speech follows, producing an uncanny, supernatural effect (the human and animal worlds momentarily touch as frog and forester comprehend each other's words), and the opera closes with a triumphal reprise of the melody of Sharp-Ears's words to Golden-Stripe ("Wait, wait, we'll talk about it in Maytime"). As the orchestra pours out the phrase in hymnlike splendor, Janacek's and Tesnohlidek's message comes through with startling clarity: there is no death in nature, only continually renewed life.

Janacek's opera had its premiere in Brno on Thursday, November 6, 1924. Wrote Marie Stejskalova: "He would return home from rehearsals laughing at how the singers were learning to crawl on all fours. *Sharp-Ears* was so beautiful that even the master was surprised. I was told that at the dress rehearsal, at the end of the third act when the forester dreams about little Sharp-Ears and, instead, catches the frog, the master was weeping and told the director, Zitek, who was standing beside him, 'This you have to play for me at my funeral.'"

On August 6, 1928, Janacek walked the forest paths near Hukvaldy, became overheated, and caught a cold. Six days later he was dead from pneumonia, and his wish came true: his funeral took place on the stage of Brno's Mahen Theater, and the final scene of *The Cunning Little Vixen* sang him to his rest.

Janacek's opera has been moving through the world ever since, while Tesnohlidek's story—until now available only in Czech—has remained unknown to non-Czechs. For those able to read Tesnohlidek's novel, though, Sharp-Ears has never needed music to race into life and mischief. More than one admirer of the vixen has made the pilgrimage to the forests of the Moravsky Kras and to the village of Hukvaldy, where ancient trees and open fields still exist, and where, one likes to think, a blessed fox family still waits at the side of their eternally dozing fox mama.

If one strolls the forest paths of the Hukvaldy game preserve, one suddenly encounters a clearing where a pile of boulders stands, surrounded by a weathered picket fence. Behind the fence the ground is swept clean, the way Czechs sweep the graves of those they love, and is dotted with tributes of fresh flowers. Atop the largest boulder perches the vixen, winsome and wary, her oddly feminine wildness captured in enduring bronze.

She looks rather pleased with herself, that wonderful bronze vixen, and one can imagine her barking: "I smile and I laugh and I sing because spring is coming, wandering somewhere behind these woods and looking for the path to us! Wait! Wait! We'll talk about it in Maytime . . ."

The illustrations for this edition of *The Cunning Little Vixen* are taken from the original designs and watercolors that Maurice Sendak created for the New York City Opera production of Janacek's opera, which was directed by Frank Corsaro and had its first performance on April 9, 1981.

184

They replace Stanislav Lolek's drawings, charming but derivative pictures by an artist then in his student period. Lolek's work is swift and simple, while Tesnohlidek's story added layers of poetry and meaning; Janacek's opera delved even deeper into mood and mystery. Sendak's vision of the novel/opera manages to combine Lolek's lightness, Tesnohlidek's pantheism, and Janacek's humanity in a way possible only for an artist who has experienced all three stages in the development of Vixen Sharp-Ears.

Czech is the native language of both Tatiana Firkusny and Maritza Morgan. Each of them prepared a separate literal translation of Tesnohlidek's novel, and I based the final English text on their work. All three of us have wrestled with an unsolvable problem: the novel is written in the Moravian dialect of Brno, a patois of immense charm but great difficulty even to Czechs. Czech editions of the novel contain sizable glossaries of odd spellings and archaic words, many of them not heard even in Brno for a good half century.

We have made no attempt to reproduce Brnian dialect in English, nor have we resorted to another regional accent as a substitute. Sharp-Ears as a Cockney, a cowgirl, or a hillbilly would be absurd, and possibly unreadable as well. Besides, we feel the story transcends time and place. In our version, Tesnohlidek's characters speak colloquial English just as they speak colloquial, albeit Brnian, Czech.

As in any translation, idioms have had to be found or invented to replace those that make no sense, convey the wrong idea, or simply fall flat when rendered literally. The many double meanings, some of them risqué, which are a feature of Tesnohlidek's style, have presented mercifully few problems.

A more serious problem has been the translation of curses and other expressions of anger. English is not rich in maledictions; beyond exclamations involving excrement and odd sexual exercises, beyond limp appeals to the Almighty to disturb the peace of someone's immortal soul, English simply lacks the color and variety to express what Tesnohlidek's Moravian peasants express all too clearly. The best we could come up with for the forester's perpetual *Sakra pes!* is "Dog damn it," which does have force and a certain country flavor. But *Sakra pes* literally means "Holy dog," and while that sounds merely silly in English, it is suitably shocking to a Catholic, Middle European peasant, for it swiftly reduces everything holy to the level of the kennel. Likewise, the mosquito's *Sakva* is a baby-talk corruption of *Sakra* ("holy" twisted to imply "damn"), and, admittedly, it translates weakly as "Golly." After discarding many weaker alternatives, we settled for "golly" and went on with the story.

Several people were especially helpful to our efforts. Mrs. Alena Nemcova of the Music Information Service in Brno provided valuable source material and, with a patience that seemed limitless, scrutinized our manuscripts and answered numerous telegrams, often at her own expense. Nor could we have done without Dr. Joseph Costelli and Dr. Vladimir Krajina, who verified our references to botany and biology. Finally, we owe thanks to Dorothy Spelman and Morgan Rollins, cold-eyed proofreaders who combed grammatical fleas from our *Vixen*'s pages.

These problems having been more or less surmounted, we believe this first translation of *The Cunning Little Vixen* is as close to Tesnohlidek's original as one can get while remaining both readable and entertaining. Above all, we have tried to bear in mind that Rudolf Tesnohlidek was a professional newspaperman, and a good one, and that his novel was a huge success in a popular newspaper aimed at a mass audience.

That is the way we have tried to present it here.

Robert T. Jones
New York
1985